Betty's Chronicles of Glim Glumswick

By

Spike Brown

Illustrations by Sharon Maynard Burrows

Tower Bridge
Books

Tower Bridge Books

Copyright © 2024 by Spike Brown
Illustrations Copyright © 2024
Sharon Maynard-Burrows
Cover image by Karl Whiteley 2024

First published in 2024

A catalogue record of this book is available from
the British Library

For

Colleen & Sharon

CHAPTER

Upon the next occasion the Zmunxs' cottage chimneys needed to be swept of accumulated birds' nests and coal fire debris, Mr Arkwright arrived in jolly form. Whistling

all the while, pushing his handcart down the lane, loaded with grades of shovel, long-poled brushes, ladders and tarpaulin sheets.

While he took his tea break in the parlour, the sweep related the following true event which occurred when he was but a youth apprenticed to a Mr Todd of Fernley Dole.

"Betty, I was younger then, mebbe fourteen. Fernley Dole is, as you know, a hamlet the other side of Woolminster dominated then, as now, by the big house, a Palladian mansion belonging to the Alford family. Each May, us sweeps from the county, a blacker and filthier mob as ever seen at one gathering, got together to bang shovels and hammers, metal lids, creating havoc, following in procession our Jack-o'-the-Green. A tall wicker figure robed in evergreens, crowned by a garland of flowers. The procession included the Giants, the

Morris Sides, the Bogeys, Black Sal and Ol' Nick on a donkey.

"'The labouring class outreach themselves. I don't want those dirty, stinky fellows, the drunken and disorderly sweeps, parading in our hamlet anymore,' said Her Ladyship one May morn to he who owned all the land and estates for miles, the lord of the manor, Henry Alford. "Tis not Christian - it harks back to a time of green giants, goblins, sacrifice of maidens and worship of pagan gods. You must stop this festival... ban it. You *will* stop it, Lord Alford. Fernley Dole must be free of this vile Jack- o'-the-Green excitement, this loathsome tour from one public house to another, both rowdy and lecherous. Well, Henry?"

"You are, of course, right, my dear. I shall put a stop to it this instant."

"Thus, for the first time in a century or more, the parade of the Worshipful Company of Chimney

Sweeps was banned and a magistrate's order obtained. What could we do? Them's at the big house could do what they liked, we were just scum. But ... but Betty, on the eve of Jack- o'-the-Green, a strange fate befell the Lady Alford. For denying our wicker man his yearly outing she paid with her life.

"Mr Todd, my employer, and I were knocked up at the sweep's house, a servant sent by his grieving master to fetch us. What misery, for during the high winds, the gales that raged all day over the county, Her Ladyship had been seated, as was her custom, before the great fireplace attending to

her embroidery when, in an instant, a tiny skull came hurtling down the chimney, crashing into the grate amongst the burning coals. The skull seemed to grin at her, rapidly growing redder and hotter, glowing the more fiercely in the roaring flame. "Such was the shock, that the Lady Alford collapsed and died on the spot of a heart failure, terror spoiling her once attractive womanly features. I tell you truthfully, Betty, Lord Alford, now a widower on the eve of Jack-o'-the-Green, showed us the very fireplace, the tiny grinning skull still in place, central to the heaped coal ash. "

"Tis devilry, sir. What am I to make of this blasphemous monstrosity sent from some pagan realm? Well, Mr Todd, have you any view? My poor deceased wife awaits the vault, resting within her studded, lead-lined coffin in the chapel as we speak.'

"Without further ado, Mr Todd charged me, his apprentice, to poke long poles up the chimney and be prepared for a retrieval.

"'Lord Alford, sir, I offer my condolences,' my employer said, humbly holding his filthy, greasy cap in his even grubbier hands, his clothes and face, like mine, black with coal grime, proud of the fact we hardly ever washed.

"'I fear, in another age to our own, a master sweep like myself ordered his climbing boy to ascend this vast chimney belonging to Your Lordship's magnificent Palladian mansion set as it is in acres of park. Alas, the boy became awkwardly stuck, killed by an avalanche of soot, asphyxiating him along one of the bends. May God forgive me, for he, the master sweep, concerned only with pocketing his fee, not wishing to face criminal proceedings for negligence, nor the bother of knocking a wall down to retrieve the body, bearing in mind the extra cost to His

Lordship, decides to leave the poor child's corpse high up where it was. Over time, it had turned into a decayed skeleton and the high winds finally dislodged the heap of bones, causing the child's skull to fall down the wide chimney into the grate. Lord save us, sir. Bless Your Lordship. Like your dear, departed wife, the Lady Alford, at least bestow a kindly boon. Allow these paltry remains of a destitute pauper a decent Christian burial in yonder green and pleasant churchyard.'

"'Zounds,' His Lordship sneered, unable to conceal his disapproval, full of utter contempt for such a suggestion. 'On the north side perhaps, wherein lie the unmarked graves of paupers, suicides and plague victims; that will do well enough, yet still I have but a wiser course. Let the skeleton be hung whole, wired well, as a classroom exhibit for the betterment of science.'"

"Oh, Mr Arkwright," sighed Betty Zmunx, enjoying the strange account of true-life events. "I should so like to discover a mysterious skull for myself."

"Are you going to Professor Lallington's lecture on the historic Glumswick Ley Line at the village hall," said Mother, swiftly changing the subject continuing work at her crochet over by the stove. "Try to stop me," insisted Aunt Medley, "did you know those two old dames Prissy Lloyd and Mags Gray, the very worst gossips in Glim Glumswick were at the village post office, boasting which of their apple pies is going to win the church bake."

So I Said
Never!

CHAPTER

etty Zmunx was travelling back by train from Woolbridge halt where there was a gravel pit and, on higher ground, a woodland trail. The local newspaper carried an article that week concerning the Glim Glumswick Archaeological Society which was in the process of carrying out a dig in the area to locate traces of an early Bronze Age settlement. Joining her on the day out to the gravel pit was Winnie White and best friend Lizzie.

Whilst the two carriages - with clerestory roofs, a raised central section, compartments lit when dark by compressed oil gas - rattled along, Winnie raised her eyes to the luggage rack and, for the first time, spied an item that must have been left behind by somebody.

"Oh, do look, you lot," she exclaimed, jumping up, "a hatbox, a pretty ordinary one, somebody left it in the corner, forgot to take it with them. Betty, stand on the seat and fetch it down, we must look inside. Is there a label, a name, something of the owner?"

Clambering over the cloth-covered seat, despite the carriage lurching, Betty managed to cling onto the wire rack, stretching out her arm to nudge the hatbox further towards her, passing it down carefully to Lizzie, the tallest of the trio, who in turn handed it to Winnie, the shortest.

The girls huddled round. Admittedly, the hatbox looked fairly battered, the outer silk threadbare, worn in places. Winnie, propping her knee on the seat, lifted the hatbox lid, everyone eager to see what lay inside - a 'poke' bonnet, a trendy cloche or chimney pot hat like Betty wore? Nothing like that - a human skull.

Betty Zmunx lost no time lifting it out and twirling it round like Hamlet. But, face it, a skull, however hard we try to think about it, looks just like a zillion others buried in cemeteries and churchyards all over Britain. How this one came to be left in a hatbox on a passenger train was certainly queer, though.

The girls were perhaps naturally inquisitive.

Scared? No, definitely not. The sun was shining; it was a lovely summer's day, motes of floating dust, bars of bright sunlight filling the compartment.

"Poor old 'Skully', he looks ever so sorry for himself," said Winnie, patting the chalky white dome, the cranium.

"That's if it's a 'he' and not a 'she'," pointed out Betty.

She peered at the inner lining of the hatbox, noting paint stains, long dried - most likely caused by a painter's brushes, a palate knife, leaky tubes of paint - so she quickly surmised the hatbox could have belonged to an artist travelling on the train, an artist who preferred to paint in oils, carried the old hatbox along with a portable easel when outdoors. All speculation, mind.

"I suppose we'd better hand it in at the station, the Parcels Office, Lost Property," suggested Winnie, anxious to be good and sensible. "'Skully' does look awfully glum."

Betty had another more daring proposition. "Hang it all, Winnie. I know just the person who could help. I mean, if it's prehistoric belonging to a hairy chimp man or ape-man, whatever."

"Oh," exclaimed Lizzie, not really sure, replacing the skull in the hatbox, for the stopping service was presently coming into Glim Glumswick station. Winnie re-secured the lid, but was more determined than ever to be good, to do right.

"We'd better just hand it in," said she, primly as could be. "It's not our property, after all. Someone may want to claim it."

"No," insisted Betty. "We must take it to an expert."

Once away from the station, the girls called to see Professor Lallington, whom Betty first knew when the kindly chappie had been a great help to her, one of his local history books in the public library being crucial to solving a village mystery.

He was, in fact, the nearest personality Betty could equate locally as being akin to A.C. Doyle's Sherlock Holmes. Alright, perhaps an older, salt-and-pepper-haired version, but the professor had the requisite hawk-like features, was very tall and lanky, and sometimes wore a dressing gown when pottering around indoors. His favourite choice of tobacco pipes was a curved meerschaum, the bowl carved in the shape of a gargoyle.

Professor Lallington was at home busy writing his next folklore volume, ensconced in his cramped, book-lined study, when the trio called. He welcomed them wholeheartedly, requesting his trusty Mrs Hurlingstone to fetch a cooling jug of Robertson's lemon barley water and the biscuit barrel.

"Now, my dears," said he, sitting them all down. "I observe a perfectly ordinary black hatbox, somewhat battered, of long usage. However, its contents are, I presume, of singular significance. That's it, drink your barley water. Betty, what have you got to tell me?"

"Well, Professor, we found it on the train. It had been left behind on the luggage rack."

"A human skull," he said, prising off the lid, adjusting his round spectacles. He lit his pipe, pondering the object.

"Is 'Skully' prehistoric?" queried Winnie politely, putting her empty glass on the arm of the chair.

"Neanderthal? No, I think not. Bronze Age far

more of a possibility," said he, glowering in her direction. "We have our Bronze Age burial mound, just outside the village and of course the GLUMSWICK LEY LINE continuing to provoke debate."

"Could somebody have been travelling with the hatbox from the gravel pit?" asked Lizzie.

"Sharp, very astute. You infer an anthropologist, a member of the British palaeontological community? A plausible theory that holds much merit, certainly, but let us consider the skull's actual age. Might I carry out a number of tests, a chemistry experiment, Betty? We must use every method open to us, be unafraid of modernity."

"Oh, do, please do," she answered, so delighted to see the gentleman kept a table available over by the window, littered with all manner of chemistry paraphernalia: a colourful display of crystals and liquids, racks of oddly shaped crucibles, test tubes, retorts and further useful apparatus, a Bunsen burner close to hand, just like Sherlock at 221B used to create his own stinks. This was just too good to be true. Perhaps she might regard the professor as a close relation to the great consulting detective.

Whatever, the girls gathered round to watch. Ten minutes later, the professor was ready.

"Humph," said he, talking more to himself than his captive audience. "A most edifying development. I concur the skull was cunningly soaked in a solution of potassium dichromate to produce a realistic patina, an ageing effect. It may even have been boiled in an iron sulphate solution. We can therefore discount its Simian origins as entirely bogus."

"What does all that mean, please?" asked Lizzie.

"Well, my dear, I believe this to be a human skull closer to our own time, faked to appear much older."

Professor Lallington wished to perform more tests, so it was unanimously agreed he should keep the skull till Monday. He would also make a forensic study of the worn hatbox, then all parties should confer as to what further steps should be taken.

Later that evening, the girls were gathered in Betty's bedroom beneath the eaves and sweet-smelling thatch, the skull mystery becoming more and more intriguing.

"Suppose, just suppose, the hatbox belonged to an artist, a painter who used the hatbox for convenience to store brushes and tubes."

"Only one way to find out," admitted Betty, sat upon the edge of her bed. Recalling a Sherlock adventure, she had read in mother's latest edition of the *Strand Magazine*. Maybe she should adopt one of Holmes' tried and tested methods that got results fast. AN ADVERTISEMENT. This one placed in the *Glim Glumswick Echo*:

Lost and Found

Artist's hatbox left on train.

Please contact Mr Lallington,

No. 6 Old Pasture Lane for safe return.

On the Tuesday, a lady called at the professor's country cottage. She was refined, elegant and impeccably turned out. She was a professional artist, a member of the Royal Academy who had enjoyed exhibitions both here and abroad: her name - Maggie Swinfen.

"Oh, how kind of you. Silly me. I was weighed down with shopping bags and totally forgot my old hatbox. I left it on the rack the other day. Let's see, a shilling each. Thank the girls ever so for bothering. My friend, Mr Hoad, lent me the artefact for a composition I intend to sketch. The skull has been in his family for years. A notorious hoax whereby his naughty great-grandfather attempted to dupe the Natural History Society, fobbing it off as a genuine prehistoric find, when, in point of fact, it was a fake. He was deservedly rapped on the knuckles and suffered ridicule from fellow club members for many years afterwards."

CHAPTER

3

Best Doggy Ever

Shelling peas under the shade of an ash tree, surrounded by colourful herbaceous borders in the sunny garden Aunt enthused, "Oh, t'was a lovely occasion," Betty knelt beside her on the lawn cradling an enormous bowl full of shredded pods, oblivious to a couple of wasps buzzing inquisitively about her straw bonnet - about to settle.

Her aunt was not slow to act; she shooed them off with a folded *Times* newspaper. But wasps are tenacious, and for some reason Betty had attracted the insects and they were soon back.

"A stout oaken coffin, you see. The handles cleverly carved in the shape of doggy's paws. Wonderful, and even a brass nameplate screwed to the lid. Old Beezer, bless his cotton socks, certainly received a terrific send off. The dog was buried at the back of the garden by the holly hedge."

"What was he exactly, Auntie? He was very big ... bigger than most dogs I've ever seen in the village."

Aunt Medley paused at her task, smiling at the memory. "Beezer is what is commonly referred to as a cross, Betty - that is, between a Labrador and a Newfoundland. That gave him his strength and that build; tall as a man when stood on his legs, but the temperament - oh, the sweetest, gentlest, kindest nature. Children like yourself, my dear, simply adored him whenever he was desirous of trotting into the village from his kennel at Railway Cottage to see everybody and woof hello."

"Mr Nincolme Poopson is a carpenter? A woodworker?"

"Yes, rather a splendid one. Your doll's house was built by him, but his day job is in charge of the signal box on the Wellingford branch. I'm sure he will miss poor old Beezer for company in his cabin. Drat those

beastly wasps, we'd better hurry indoors. Another three of them, that's five. The nest must be nearby. We don't want to get stung and our faces to swell. Wasps have vicious stings. Bumble bees are alright in the garden, but not those things. I shall contact Mr Fuller."

Betty and her aunt joined Mother in the cool of the spacious drawing room upon a comfy sofa before a large brick settle, the fireplace hung with various horse brasses, decorative bellows and fire tongs. An inlaid cabinet stood beneath the window atop of which a porcelain milkmaid, vase of flowers and a very big bowl for fruit presided. To one side of the fireplace was a wrought-iron lamp standard, and a brass vase sufficed for umbrellas over by the stable-style front door.

"Wasps," Aunt Medley reminded everyone, ordering tea from their domestic, Mrs Appleton, "on the attack, ready to sting."

"Oh dear, that is a nuisance," said Mother, glancing up from her crochet. "I expect there's a nest in the orchard that needs smoking out. Mr Fuller is our man. Betty, would you help Mrs Appleton with the tea things, darling? There's a good girl."

***

Betty and Aunt Medley were coming out of the pharmacist along the village High Street, only to bump into Mr Poopson who had been delivering a number of his wooden flower tub creations to Faringdon's, the local ironmonger; the High Street retailer could not sell them quickly enough. The decorative windmill and wheelbarrow tubs proving so popular.

"Why, bless 'ee, Miss Medley, an' you too, young Betty. Yer liked the doggy fooneral, eh, ma'am?"

"Very fitting," replied the aunt. "The vicar spoke

so eloquently, such a lovely sunny morning. Do you miss Beezer? Of course, you must."

"Allus I does, ma'am, but the ol' boy, 'oweffer pop'lar wi' folk, wuzz very ancient boned and arfritick, so it were for the best. However, 'e ... erm ..." The signalman paused in mid-sentence, licking his lips, a glazed look in his eyes.

"Do go on, Mr Poopson."

"I don't knows I should, ma'am, but, er ..."

"Do stop procrastinating. Out with it, man!" Aunt Medley put down her shopping bag, a reassuring smile enough to prompt a response.

"I seen 'im these three times, Miss Medley. T'were getting dark, see, twilight, like as not. Luss evening I wuzz waterin' the borders in the garden at my cottage, thinking 'bout my supper, I 'ad a nice stew and dumplin's planned, then I 'ears barking familiar t'me over by the holly hedge. Fer a flash, there be me dear old dog jest as afore, waggin' 'is tail, tongue 'anging out. Jest normal, like, but 'e weren't normal wuzz 'e - couldn't been."

Mr Nincolme Poopson had managed the same signal box all his working life. Although paid less than his main-line counterpart - due to having far fewer trains - he often earned pocket money repairing bicycles, rabbiting, building little garden windmills and flower tub wheelbarrows, and generally putting his woodworking skills to good use between trains. He had a responsible job and needed to keep his eye on the signal, the instruments in his cabin and the crossing gates. Old Beezer had been well known to railway men on the line and his large wolfish presence at the station should be missed by passengers, for he quite freely roamed the platform and waiting rooms and was appreciated. Now he had a little, crafted wood cross up by the holly hedge.

****

Young Miss Zmunx and her companion, Lizzie Meredith, bumped into their friends, Lucian Finn and Basil Thyme, at the school gates. Lucian, the undisputed conker champion, was a bit of a swot who, when he grew up, had no desire to become an engine driver, but wanted to join the library service and one day become custodian of Glim Glumswick public library. Basil was the undisputed king of swots who came first in class at everything.

They went for tea and an iced bun at the teashop, Betty taking the lead suggesting that they take up the strange matter of the undead dog.

"Betty," said Basil, "you were brilliant in that *Lost Stradivarius Mystery*, in which you solved a mystery, but what puzzle draws you into this dog-haunting nonsense? Clearly Mr Poopson is off his top, a bit of a loony, wouldn't you agree?"

"I would," said Lucian confidently.

"So would I," agreed Lizzie.

"But it *is* a puzzle, don't you see?" insisted the young girl vehemently.

"That's just it, with this ghost whatnot," continued Basil, "I mean, suppose after Beezer died and was buried, Mr Poopson, in his imagination, willed him back, but not really. I mean, the dog don't sound that ghostly. I'd expect *the hound of death* to be absolutely RABID: red-eyed, snarling, fangs dripping blood."

***

"Well, I must say, yorn a 'sceptical spectacles', ain't yer, Basil? I didna imagine nuffink. Tell ya what, I dare you children to stay in the garden when it starts to git dark, an' see fer yerselves I ain't fibbing," insisted Mr Poopson, puffing on his pipe.

The signalman checked the special railway time clock above the mantelshelf in his cabin surrounded by his telegraph machines and the polished row of levers he pulled with a cloth to change the signals. Everyone was drinking tea out of chipped mugs. A bell pinged, a train was due. The fun of being so close to the railway track, and to see a steam train approach, was exciting and engrossing for the boys

Lucian Finn and Basil Thyme, but Betty was far more concerned about the ghost-dog puzzle.

"I'm going to Mr Poopsons' garden. Coming Lizzie?"

"Alright."

The girls climbed back down the signal box steps to the cinder path and made their way along beside the tracks to Railway Cottage where the signalman lived. A train whistle hooted in the distance round the curve.

'But why,' thought Betty to herself, 'why does the ever-faithful Beezer show himself like this - return from the grave? Not to scare anyone, it seems.'

The first clue was provided when Betty happened to notice an oxidised green coin nestling in the shorn tufts of grass just past the vegetable plot. Suddenly, a loud barking started up from behind the nearby holly hedge, making the girls jump, nearly scream and run for their lives. Could it be Beezer, the ghostly giant dog, the hound of death? Dr Lent, the village G.P. appeared, wearing his tweed cap and plus fours and shiny brown brogues. A tiny bundle of fur scampered from behind the hedge - it was a Chihuahua. What a loud and raucous bark it had for such a small animal. Quite unnerving, in fact, but the barking certainly didn't belong to Beezer, the ghost-dog haunting the garden at Railway Cottage.

"Hello, Betty Zmunx, and you Lizzie," apologised the local medical practitioner, scooping up his little dog. "Queenie was very naughty and ran off up the woodland footpath, got under the fence of Mr Poopsons' garden, but I've got her now. Good evening to you both."

He doffed his cap and returned into the woods, crashing through the undergrowth, beating it back with his stout ash stick until he attained the fence just as a train further down went chuffing past the cottage into the station proper.

The girls came hurrying back up the timber steps to the signal box. Mr Poopson was smoking his pipe, brewing more tea in the pot. The boys were playing Snap at the table.

"Mr Poopson, Mr Poopson!" Betty gasped, bursting into the cabin, her face flushed, all blotchy. "Beezer wanted you to look at the holly hedge, to dig it up. That's why he came back as a ghost. Honestly, I found these old coins scattered under the bush, amongst the roots, six of them, a treasure trove!"

The signalman considered one of the coins in the palm of his grubby hand. "Aye, s'pose so. Alrigh', Betty, I'll pop over between trains an' fetch me spade and pitchfork. The boys'll 'elp. I need a bit o' rope to drag that hedge outta ground, tug o'war, like as not."

Thus, to the children's delight, a veritable hoard of gold was discovered that evening at twilight: Roman coins, necklets and goblets tracing back to pagan times.

Incredibly, Beezer's ghost was responsible for Mr Poopson being in pocket to the tune of one hundred pounds when the Roman treasure was later sold to

the British Museum by Mr Smith, a local historian and stalwart member of the Glim Glumswick Archaeological Society.

CHAPTER 4

Ink Spots

The exasperated bank manager, Mr Herbert Andrews, offering a plate of pastry fruit tartlets for the delectation of Aunt Medley and Betty, asked quite honestly," how was it done?" The tea rooms along the high street were as usual crowded and bustling with conversation, mostly ladies' gossip. Mr Andrews was a church member who sang bass in the choir, hence they were friends. "My light grey frock coat was ruined and looked unsightly, spotted with ink, but the room was locked, I say, the windows barred. I was sat at my desk, alone, dealing with a large deposit of cash, no one else in the room apart from myself, so how did the darned ink spots get there? How exactly was it done?"

"A puzzler to be sure," admitted the aunt. "Alas, my own intellect should be found wanting to consider this business of ink spots, but Betty, my niece, might be better able to find an explanation. She is rather clever at mysteries, aren't you, dear?"

"Indeed," the fellow butted in. "I am assured of your reputation, Miss Betty: 'Trip to Hamleys, 'The Message in a Book' being amongst your early successes," agreed the bank manager smugly, ingratiating himself. "And yet this matter of my ruined frock coat may yet prove too formidable. Your age, I refer to; you are but a juvenile."

"I don't think so," said Betty, daintily placing a fruit tartlet in her mouth.

"You don't think so?" said he doubtfully. "Well, I, an adult, just have no idea. All I know is that when I walked into the room my frock coat was impeccably clean and pressed, and when I came back out again, bank staff were sniggering behind my back. My head clerk, Mr Dunn, pointed out the stains; we thus sought out the cloakroom's full length mirror."

"But Mr Andrews, you're absolutely certain the ink spots were not there before you entered the room and locked the door behind you? You just hadn't noticed?" Betty Zmunx queried.

"Well, my girl, you see I can vouch for this. Earlier, just before I entered the room in question, I used a clothes brush to dust off my coat. Mr Dunn assisted, no marks were then in evidence. The mirror did not lie, neither when I passed the counter, or clerks at work, did I hear one snigger when my back was turned. Mr Dunn assures me my coat was perfectly spotless before I entered the room with the cash box."

"Perhaps my niece could see the room?

Accompanied by myself, of course," suggested Aunt Medley, Betty in full agreement, sipping her Earl Grey.

"Why, Miss Medley, after we have polished off this most delicious repast of tea and cakes, we shall visit the bank at once. The City & Counties Bank should be honoured. Now, if I might draw your attention to the church bazaar of the 14th. The entrance fee, I believe, should be raised from a halfpenny to a penny. What, as a committee member, are your thoughts?"

***

The room proved exactly as described - functional. The windows barred, furniture consisting of the bank manager's desk and swivel chair, a small coffee table, a safe, a filing cabinet in one corner, the walls tastefully decorated by a number of water colours, but, most pertinently, Betty Zmunx focused on a large, Swiss, cherry- brown cuckoo clock carved with squirrels, birds and leaves. Tiny doors above a gold clock face displaying Roman numerals sprung open on the hour. The wall clock was hung directly behind where Mr Andrews normally leant over his desk, his back exposed, when dealing with everyday duties such as opening mail, signing letters concerned with clients' money.

While Aunt Medley and Mr Andrews were busy discussing church matters, Betty sidled over to where the cuckoo clock was placed, chains hooked with wooden dangling fir cones. It was nearly three o'clock and this proved fortuitous.

"Why, what a dull old, tired cuckoo, the spring mechanism must have wound down," exclaimed Aunt Medley, pausing from her conversation to listen, the bank manager paying little heed.

"Needs windin', s'pect," said he.

Shooh, shooh, shooh, shooh, hooooooh - the mechanical cuckoo did sound decidedly flat and slow, not its usual chirpy self. But by now, Betty, blessed with a real talent for observing almost insignificant details, had noticed a scrunched-up ink pellet - normally flicked in class by means of a rubber band at a person sat in front of you, or in the next row - hidden over by the wastebasket. The coffee table, she quickly realised, had been shifted across the carpet so someone of her height, perhaps a bit taller, could reach up and, by opening the little double doors, tamper with the cuckoo clock by winding the hour hand so a pellet could be ingenuously incorporated in the spring mechanism, the inky missile to be propelled exactly on the hour when the cuckoo sprang forth, from that angle easily able to strike the back of the bank manager's pristine, light-grey frock coat and splat it with ink while he worked at his desk, so that when Mr

Andrews left the room, he should be open to ridicule.

Making sure the adults were not looking, the girl snatched the pellet off the carpet, placing it in her jacket pocket, no one any the wiser, but she, Betty Zmunx, now had a good idea who was the mischief maker responsible.

"What a pity you could not solve the mystery of the locked room, Betty. Now that really is a puzzle worthy of your Sherlock by A.C. Doyle, but you're still only eleven, dear. Who knows, in time and with more experience under your belt..."

"Really," replied the girl with a smile.

Later, Betty saw young Alex Ginn swaggering along the sunny pavement like he owned Glim Glumswick. He paused to catch his reflection in the front window of Pellow's Fishing Tackle Shop, he was fourteen, recently left school to become a messenger employed in the bank's post room and it was Friday payday.

"Suspect number 1," Betty quickly put two & two together. Alex had every opportunity to plant the inky pellet. He was the perfect candidate, why, because *a post boy is free to enter departments including the bank manager's office collecting mail even if he's out.*

Seeing Winnie waving on the opposite side of the street – she quickly crossed the road and thought no more about it.

CHAPTER

Choccy Shocker

arna Amberley, whose formidable, scary Grandmother ruled Mulberry Manor, where at the end of the garden, the ghost girl and coffin pilot Tudor Sefton resided asked very politely, "I'd like a chocolate cigar please." How the Grandma hated her house and grounds being haunted by that pesky spirit and had even hired a so called 'psychic exterminator', to get rid of Tudor – all to no avail, and apparently the ghost girl was now bestest friends with Larna and Betty Zmunx, which made the old lady even more annoyed.

"There has been a frightful murder," said Mrs Staple, proprietor of the village sweet shop.

"Oh," said Betty curiously, her voice guarded. "Do tell." The girl chose a half dozen lemon drops for her own after-school treat.

"Terrible, awful it were. The head all cracked."

"Yuk," sighed Larna, unwrapping the foil from her chocolate cigar, offering Betty a withering glance before stepping out of the shop into the sunshine to join her pals, a motor car and a delivery van whizzing past.

"It'll be the third to be done away with in that manner," Mrs Staple murmured.

"All chocolate rabbits?" asked the girl, helping herself to a sweet from the bag.

"Aye. What's to be done, Miss Betty? I'm mystified, I really am."

It must be admitted, young Miss Zmunx was up for the challenge since so brilliantly solving *the Hat Box Mystery* that summer, offering a very plausible and rational explanation that the village constable, no less, should have been hard put to equal. She was always happy when an opportunity arose to test her.

I mean, chocolate rabbits, for goodness sake. Mrs Staple was widely regarded in the village as thick as two planks, a bit vacant, but there was promise here, potential to employ her wits to good advantage.'

"If I solve this, Mrs Staple, I should quite like two free boxes of those Fry's mint creams: one for my Aunt Medley and one for my mother."

"Why, child, bless yer. It shall be done. I'm losing stock, see. Allus can't stock killed chocolate rabbits with their heads bashed in, now can I?"

Before leaving with her bag of sweets, Betty noticed a *mousetrap* the other side of the counter, positioned along the skirting board, the wire engaged, a tiny scrap of cheese in place. High above, a narrow shelf ran along the wall full of chocolate rabbits. This prompted the little girl to call on Miss Nedlow, whose cottage backed onto the shop, separated by a wall and garden in full riotous bloom. She walked briskly and in no time was using her balled fist to rap against the front door.

"Yes, Betty. What can I do, dear? Are your aunt and mother well?"

"Very. I wondered, Miss Nedlow, if I might earn a penny doing a gardening errand."

"Such a kindness. I do have a little weeding in the flower borders needs doing, and while you're about it, you might like to water the pots. You dip your can in the rusty water tank beside the glasshouse. You know how it's done by now. My servant, Molly, shall prepare lemonade."

"Oh, thank you, Miss Nedlow."

"Betty, here, remove your ribboned school bonnet and put on this straw hat, child, to protect you from the heat."

The hot, clammy weather was, in part, responsible for the sweet shop murders, Betty thought as she walked up the sunny garden.

At the end where the knapped flint wall was situated, she borrowed a wooden crate and, stood on tiptoe, was able to consider the view, taking into account the wide-open rear windows of Mrs Staple's house across the way.

At night, because it was so humid, folk in the village, including the sweet shop owner, would keep their windows halfway, or a quarter, open to allow for cooling air. The parlour at the back led along the hall directly to the shop. A sill, not too far up, thus made it easily accessible.

***

"Goodness, this box of mint confection is really most thoughtful, and you say you solved three murders, all by the end of the afternoon. Shouldn't you have asked permission from Constable Johns at the police house first? Doesn't the local force at Wellingford normally deal with serious crime?" queried Aunt Medley.

"Betty, I'm delighted with my box of chocolate creams," said her mother, proudly glancing up from her knitting, sat beside the homely hearth.

"I think you're very clever. Well, tell us, child, what happened. Who got arrested?"

"No one got arrested, exactly," Betty answered, knelt beside her mother, holding a ball of wool. "I mean, you can't arrest a cat for chasing a mouse, can you?"

"Can't you, dear?" frowned Aunt Medley. "A naughty one deserves to be."

CHAPTER

6

Case For Fairies

Betty and Larna stood outside the vault of their dearest ghost friend down the end of Mulberry Manor's Garden.

"What a crackerjack time," Gushed Larna Amberly. "That old silver casket you're after Tudor, I heard all the doors banging, the books being moved about and that suit of armour crashing down, waking Grandma - your ghostly self-up and about. She was purple livid!"

"Oh, but I never found it - where can my old family heirloom have got to? I've been searching the manor for what must be centuries b'now."

"Well," Said Betty, "It's Midsummer's Eve, maybe the fairy folk can help." She smirked.

"Now Zmunxy, you got me thinkin' gal - you're an unbeliever so far fairy's are concerned, I take it."

"Oh, me and Larna, we just love the fables by ole' Hans Anderson, but no, I never seen one properly - up close I mean."

"Well, here me out the pair of you - you know that perfect ninny Mr. Poopson, the signalman who mans the crossing gates."

"Surely we do, he's a real friend, helpful and always kind as could be."

"Well do ask him," Tudor said "About garden fairie folk I mean."

The old railwayman, in his signal box and garden fairies - the two just didn't seem to mix somehow...

＊＊＊

"Fairies, now you got me thinking." Said Mr Poopson sitting back in his creaky, worn armchair. He lit his pipe, aware of a chattering family of birds nesting in the guttering.

The signal box was his responsibility, his domain - spotlessly clean, levers polished daily, the pinging electronic telegraph machine always listened out for, the signals and instruments a priority. One lapse of memory, even on a country branch line, could spell disaster; say a tunnel collision, a goods derailment. The gated level crossing must also be operated.

Lately, he had seen many more cyclists, a small number of motors, but out here in the countryside, a rural, farming community, who needed motors? Horses were perfectly sufficient. You only had to see them in everyday use hauling ploughs, wagonettes, delivery carts, yellow-wheeled dog carts, farmers' gigs and buggies to realise equines ruled! The branch railway rightly expected to shift produce and the local populace from one place to another.

With plenty of time between trains, no passenger service or goods expected this hour of the day, the

sun beating down, shining resplendently in a deep blue sky, Mr Nincolme Poopson led the children across to his cottage.

The railwayman's garden was much admired locally, passengers prone to peer out of the carriage windows as the stopping service passed by, clay pots of geraniums on the sun-drenched patio, the upper and lower ponds, the vast array of flowers in bloom, quirky, witty garden ornaments, the waterfall, the stream, the reed beds, the honeysuckle-clematis arch, a waterwheel, mediaeval-style bridge built by Mr Poopson of stout oak, double tier rose beds shored up by sawn lengths of telegraph poles, a brick-walled pathway at the bottom. So much of interest to take in.

"The fish are very big," said Lucian, leaning forward, as they paused by the lower pond where there was a profusion of yellow lilies, bees buzzing around flower tubs on the patio.

"How they plop about, glide underwater, weaving this way and that. Oh, Mr Poopson, the water's so clear."

"Yep, that water feeds from my own well. We'll take a peep at that later - there see," He said excitedly, "Two of me fattest 'n' finest. Fred, a fifteen pound white Koi an' Tess

a seventeen pounder.

Ooh, 'ad 'em fer years.

Keeps me goldfish an'

wild carp in the top pond.

Promise you'll keep a

secret, the both of yer."

"Alright," said Lucian Finn.

"A promise is a promise," agreed Betty, meaning every word.

Seemingly satisfied, the branch signalman guided the children along the grass, past the patio ornamented with a pair of carved stone Spanish donkeys, the dwarf-sized garden hut with asphalt roof, the weather-beaten timber duck house and hatchery, the fruit trees burdened with clusters of apples, plums, and pears until they finally reached the circular brick and cemented well, intuitively dug and built by Mr Poopson single-handedly.

"Pal o' mine," said he, cheerfully, "once tol' me, an old wise country fella he were too, a water diviner it so 'appens, y'know, uses a Y-shaped twig, that I'd likely as not struck a fairy spring, the luck I had discovering this source of water too remarkable.

"'Mr Openshawe,' I laughed, slappin' him on the back, 'enough of blinkin' fairies. I've got me a wonderful free source of pure, fresh water. I'm gonna build me ponds, a miniature waterwheel, 'ave a runnin' stream, reed beds and plank bridges. Yes, I've been fortunate, certainly, but fairy folk is takin' it too far. You mean they sort of influenced me, guided me to the spot? Well, I never see'd no fairies, goblins nor elves either in me garden.' My companion showed annoyance at my nonchalant, carefree attitude.

"'But you will,' promised he, guardedly, and mind, I was respectful of Mr Openshawe, I was often privileged to shoot rabbits and pheasants with 'im, for he was head gamekeeper on Sir Winton Clarke's estates. 'Oh yes, the time will come, my lad,' said he emphatically.

"Well, Betty, no sooner had he spoke than I felt a shiver like someone had just walked over me grave. See, I'd read somewhere most fairies were capable of spreading fairy dust and good fortune to us gard'ners, but others wilful, spiteful, downright evil causin' blight and disease to plants, despisin' 'umankind ... which lot I was lumbered with I paused to wonder, but as time went by, and my garden flourished, became a beautiful haven, gettin' lovelier with each season, I knew in me 'eart I had been blessed and if, as Mr Openshawe suggested, garden fairies really existed then, why, they and their magical spring were very welcome, well fairies do exist, I've seen 'em and you will too."

***

61

After going home for a proper tea, the weather being warm and sunny, the children returned to railway cottage.

Although Mr Poopson must remain on duty at his box as arranged, Betty and the boy, took up their vantage in the garden greenhouse attached to the cottage, a giant prickly pear cactus for company.

There was a splendid view of the upper and lower ponds, and the garden in general. Midsummer's eve was on everyone's lips.

Time passed, then as the glorious silken sunset melted purple and red, the children witnessed the first remarkable happening.

A garden ornament, a hand-painted footballer, the stone figure left out in the elements for a long time, had somehow come alive. Why, he was kicking a fir cone along the grass, and such was his deft control, the footballer flicked it first onto his head - *clunk* - bounced it onto his raised knee - *donk* - and

rolled it down his leg - *duggety-duggety, dug-dug* -
onto the ground, making a very fine dribble past the
greenhouse.

A tiny whistle blew, and yet more granite garden
ornaments, this time a steam tractor driven by a
hedgehog towing a tinker's caravan. How was this
possible? After all, they were made of stone and
quite heavy.

The procession continued, including a pair of Stone Age, big- nosed trolls - man and wife - the entwined lovers, the gossips, old Tom, the snail, the cricketer, the umpire, the demon imp, the Spanish donkeys, all once solid stone figures, weighty, inanimate objects, magically transformed, clunking and scraping along merrily, hastening towards the end of the garden.

Meanwhile, high on the corner of the grassy bank, a black-and-white pig, a stone effigy, would keep squealing and grunting, all the ornaments headed in the direction of Mr Poopson' brick and concreted well. Why, all the garden ornaments, it appeared, were gathering to celebrate midsummer's eve, joining a host of pretty, fluttering fairies who entwined delicate, gossamer hands and were dancing firstly one way, then the other, round the well's perimeter, the area lit up by glow-worms.

Later, Mr Poopson came hurrying across – waving his railway lamp, the lamplight shone on the children's faces, "Now, not a word to anybody about this. The fairy folk is lovely, ever so kind, but very strict. Never, never, I say, mention about the magical doings this eventide to no one... not even your mother."

Betty's Mum

"Ooh, there goes Tudor," pointed out Betty shifting her gaze, "see, the yellowy blue light shooting across the sky. That's her lantern on a stick."

"Wow," sighed Lucian, "that's seriously fast, wish I had a flying coffin like her."

"Your 'avin me orn," laughed Mr Poopson, not believing a word, I mean fairies was pushing the boundary, but flying coffins – now that sounds plain daft.

The magic of Glim Glumswick

CHAPTER

7

Evil Potion

P.C. Johns was the village constable who lived at the police house, a cob and thatch cottage opposite the Mitre Inn.

Recently, he had been in the papers, for as Aunt Medley pointed out, he had been officially commended for bravery after arresting a house burglar, rather a violent cracksman called Alfie Nibbs who lived locally and had nine children, who was tried at Wellingford assizes and sent down for six years hard labour, the crook's wife having to be restrained in court after the verdict, the jury all of one accord, for she lashed out viciously at P.C. Johns with her handbag saying the unrepeatable. He suffered a bruised cheek but did not press charges and let her off with a caution.

"He is rather on the fat side," mentioned mother, darning a stocking in front of the cheery fire, a glass of sherry at her side, the banshee wind shrieking, rain lashing in torrents against the latticed windows of the cottage they shared, for it was, after all, the end of October and well into autumn - a time for squally gales.

"What's fat got to do with it? He is young and a first-rate community officer, and we are extremely lucky to have him as our village policeman. The last one, old P.C. Crewe, was thin and next to useless."

"Well, sister dear, largely built, well-rounded is what I meant, which reminds me ... Betty, would you, tomorrow before school, dear, providing the weather's cleared up, take some jars of home-made jam and pickle to the police house for the fat ... I

mean, P.C. Johns? He's always so generous with his ducks' eggs."

"Lizzie and Mary Meredith, who live opposite to the Nibbs family, say the grandmother is a witch, Mummy. She owns a hazel-twig broomstick and a big black cat."

"A cuddly black cat makes for a fond pet," laughed Aunt Medley. "My, you should make a fine witchfinder general to equal Matthew Hopkins. Are you to inform on Grandma Nibbs, then? What is to become of people who own more than one big black cat?"

"The witch hazel broom is ideal for sweeping paths, dear," her mother reminded. "I'm surprised you are so quick to accuse, Betty. You'll need more evidence, surely?"

"I'm not accusing anybody," sighed the little girl, "but Lizzie is my best friend."

The next morning, knocking at the front door of the policeman's cottage came no answer. Betty decided to pop round the side and leave the home-made jam on the kitchen step. When she got there, the door was actually unlatched and part open, but no one about.

Glancing up the garden, apart from the duck

house, she caught sight of a shingle-roofed shed where the fat policeman indulged his hobby for model railways. The foliage was wet and dripping after the night's windy weather, the path shiny with puddles. The door to the hut was ajar. Suddenly, she remembered it was October 31st.

The model railway took up most of the shed. Laid out on a pair of large, flat pieces of plyboard, it had a country station of printed tin, a goods yard, tunnel and bridges. Much attention to detail had been lavished on painting and modelling the landscape out of papier mâché. Tiny-scale people inhabited the station platform, sheep grazed in fields, fencing, miniature hedgerow and trees all in place.

"Mr Johns," she called out, feeling rather stupid, for he was obviously not there, but sensing, somehow, someone was present in the shed. Then, out of the corner of her eye, the girl could hardly believe what she saw - a tiny red flag waving frantically from the roof of the printed tin model signal box.

Astonishingly, the fat policeman was holding onto the chimney pot for dear life.

One hand waving the flag. Although still tubby in stature, he was more of an 0 gauge fat policeman who appeared exactly the same scale as the lead figures of passengers on their bases waiting along the platform. In fact, the red flag had been purloined from the painted guard who now had a hole in his flesh-coloured fist.

But what interested the child, causing her to pause and reflect, was the smell of pipe smoke that permeated the air. P.C. Johns' favourite tobacco pipe, the bowl still warm to the touch, rested on a brass ashtray, this upon the wooden workbench beside an upside-down, little tin locomotive, its insides being fixed; a winding key, oil can and a smattering of screwdrivers indicated Mr Johns had been disturbed while working, his three-legged stool scraped back

'What to do, what to do - the wicked grandma had something to do with this, *Alfie Nibbs' mother* protective of her son, vengeful because he had been imprisoned for six years hard labour, caught red-handed by P.C. Johns, sent down by the judge, leaving his wife to cope with nine children,' Betty

thought desperately. She screwed her eyes tightly shut, then opened them again with a start.

The shoebox! That item had not been there, under the trestle table, when she last came to visit in August with Aunt Medley, the kindly officer showing off his little prize model railway. P.C. Johns was normally tidy, everything in its place, and this helped, because the shoe box certainly seemed out of place - definitely so. Ignoring the roof of the Hornby signal box where the miniature P.C. Johns still waved his flag frantically, Betty knelt down, carefully prising open the cardboard lid. So, it was the grandma after all! Her school friend Lizzie had been right all along.

Now for the hard evidence. There inside, nestling on tissue paper, was a doll dressed up like a policeman, the uniform painstakingly stitched together, the helmet 

accurate even down to the county badge; the doll made in the image of P.C. Johns had six hat pins stuck in it.

Beside the doll was a brown glass bottle containing horrid liquid, bits of stag beetle floating about in the murky solution. 

The girl needed no prompting. She ran out of the shed and threw the bottle to the ground, dashing it to pieces on the flagstone path. She hurried back to the hut and, kneeling down, one by one, removed each sharp pin from the doll, careful not to prick herself.

P.C. Johns rapidly grew back to normal size, but too fast, for his sheer weight and bulk meant he collapsed the plyboard table, squashing his model railway.

CHAPTER

8

That Old Teapot

Returning from Wellingford by train, Betty totally absorbed reading Mary Elizabeth Braddon's *Lady Audley's Secret*, a popular detective yarn purchased at the bookshop in town, not until the loud blast of whistle as the train rounded the banked curve did she become alerted to the real world. Evidently, two elderly ladies got on at the previous halt for they sat nattering away on the cloth-covered seat opposite - bonnets and shawls, a sea of skirts.

The gas jets of the glass-shaded lamps illuminating the compartment, for it was already dark, were adequate, bright enough to read by. Plunging back into her detective novel, snippets of an ongoing topic of conversation occasionally intruded:

"Miss Ward, Emily, whatever did happen to that Spode teapot - quite valuable, you know?"

"Yes, Miss Fox, Kate," the other answered, "that blue China teapot kept in the kitchen. When we return home to Oakfield Hall, I shall continue to pursue my enquiries - I do hope it hasn't been ..."

"Stolen."

"Exactly, my dear. Do have another peppermint drop." She paused over a bag.

"I will, thank you," replied the other, primly. "The butler, Mr Molten, is getting on, of course, and inclined to be rather..."

"Absent-minded - a likely suspect - y'know, perhaps we should hire the service of a ..."

"Private detective. I've a mind to do just that, Miss Ward." And so the banter between the old ladies continued with frequent mention of Oakfield Hall, their place of residence.

When Betty next looked up from her book, the

gas-lit compartment, save for herself, was empty - the ladies no doubt alighted at the last stop.

The puffing engine prepared to enter her home station. She quickly jumped up grabbing her duck-handled brolly and string bag from the rack - stowing her copy of Lady Audley's secret for later.

***

"Oakfield Hall," Aunt Medley said thoughtfully, settling down to dinner, spooning more cauliflower cheese onto her plate, Betty helped herself to a large portion. "You have to look it up on that big map Mother gave you. Rings a bell."

"Well, it's all so jolly exciting. Since coming off my train from Wellingford this evening, I'm determined to offer my services and help the ladies find their missing teapot. I might even be rewarded."

The aunt, possessed of a sharp nose and angular,

chiselled chin, spoke cheerfully enough, but wished to temper her niece's enthusiasm.

"That's very thoughtful of you, Betty, although whether these genteel, upper-crust ladies who reside at Oakfield Hall actually want your services is another matter. I'd write a short note first - introduce yourself."

However, Zmunxy was far too impetuous a girl to seek delay. The following morning, another free day because of the mid-term school break, after poring over her large-scale map upstairs in her loft bedroom, finding at least Oakfield Park clearly marked on the ordinance survey, she decided to take to the open road, riding her peddle bike. Placing out the bird food earlier, she realised the sky was grey and overcast, the weather chilly, but cycling soon warmed you up and was an independent means of getting about.

Waving goodbye to Aunt Medley and the Zmunx's

faithful domestic, Mrs Appleton, some half hour later found her, bicycling in a determined way, fast approaching the Wormly Stowe turn off.

To her left, gripping the handlebars tightly, she bumped her bike onto the verge and, following the clay brick wall round, Betty came to a set of entrance gates, slightly ajar, set between two support posts, crowned by mossy stone balls. Here, then, must be the approach that led onto the estate, the park and grounds of Oakfield Hall. Climbing off her bicycle, the girl, wearing her favourite chimney-pot hat and cape, shod in nail-studded ankle boots, perfect for the terrain, proceeded to wheel her bright-green Raleigh with white saddle, up the sweeping gravel drive, gloomy from overhanging branches of Scots pines plus

encroaching clumps of wild and untamed rhododendron bushes.

Gears whirring an accompaniment, she gave an exultant ping on her cycle bell, fully expectant of sighting a large country house screened behind the immense and ancient yew hedge - but she was in for a shocker ... Oakfield Hall, or rather the ruin that remained, was but a burnt-out husk. A long- ago house fire of immense intensity had burnt out the upper storey, destroying the roof. The exposed herringbone-patterned brick chimneys, charred timbers, soot-smudged wattle and daub walls testimony to a blaze of some magnitude that had gutted what must have once been a Tudor manor house.

This just didn't make sense. Those pair of old ladies on the train lived here. This was their address, or rather an inner voice commented soberly *'where they had died ... the personalities of the two old ducks somehow surviving.'* Despite shooing away the thought, for a bit, Betty felt cold to the bones and very vulnerable to peculiar forces as the trees creaked and leaves rustled and blew about the overgrown lawn.

A swirling gust of wind made her anxious to get on. She took out her school exercise book and drew rough sketches of the burnt- out, gutted house, the paved walkway, the round fishponds to one side. She conjured up a mental picture of her own dolls house at home, all the tiny furniture and fittings, precious additions collected since she was seven. Betty cast herself in the role of miniature mistress of the house. WHAT IF a fire started in one of the upper storey rooms, *say the nursery due to a dropped candle setting light to fabric?* What if - what if - what if? So many 'what if's'. Suddenly, something plonked on top of her hat, an acorn bounced onto the grass at her feet. Betty smiled, she was stood beneath the sprawling foliage of an oak tree, but then she heard a distinct plop-plop-plopperty-plop from the direction of a Tudor fishpond, a round pond where they once kept tench and carp, supplying the dinner table for merrie olde England. Always alert to the signs of nature, the clues provided by the natural world, she hurried across the lawn and stooped over, seeing her wavering image staring back at her like a water sprite. The girl saw rising air bubbles -

glimpsed below the surface of the murky pond water, a giant, scaly fish, a freshwater carp that must have been very old to have grown to such a size.

The static fish floated in the shallows amongst the

reeds, its rubbery lips murmuring, its opaque fishy eyes inquisitive about something. More air bubbles surfaced, but by this time Betty had gone running off to fetch a suitable twig hooked at the end, for she had spotted a glimmer of decorative china, part hidden by the silt. After poking about, stirring up the mud, managing to snare the handle, with a gentle tug, using her twig, she coaxed the Spode teapot out of the water and placed it on the grass.

Lifting the teapot's lid, she gave out a gasp of surprise - a huge gemstone, the size of a duck's egg, the centre of a broach clustered with  diamonds lay within the hollow.

About to take it out and wipe it with her coat sleeve, a voice barked: "Stand away. Put that back in the teapot, dear, and replace the lid, if you please, Miss Zmunx. Your services are no longer required."

An elderly lady appeared from behind the tall yew hedge, her manner stern and uncompromising. Her stouter companion, brandishing her brolly menacingly, followed soon after, both women recognisable from the train.

"Just as Miss Fox and I anticipated when aware of your burgeoning reputation as a sleuth, we planned to ensnare you into our scheme - following your every move for the last week, waiting for you on the platform at Wellingford station, travelling in a separate carriage incognito to Otters halt, enticing you with talk of 'The Mystery of the Lost Teapot' that, as we hoped, you found irresistible. You have done a splendid job retrieving the teapot for us, Miss

Zmunx, and now you can go - get on that bicycle of yours and peddle out of the gates."

"Hold your bloomin' horses - I heard all that," called out a largely-built man in tweed jacket and plus fours, wearing a deerstalker, fast approaching on foot. In fact, this was the estate manager, Mr Cruft, the land thereabouts, including Oakfield Hall, belonging to Lord Sidgwick. "Stay where you are," he directed, holding the pair of binoculars he had seen them with earlier, a number of farm labourers rounding the women. "You're the people the police were after at the time. Fox and Ward, suspected of deliberate arson. Your game, pinching the Waldemar diamond belonging to the Russian Grand Duchess Kirillovna, a gift from the Tsar. You, Miss Ward, I recall were the nanny in charge of her two children - you, Miss Fox, a hired cook. At the request of Queen Victoria, the Grand Duchess stayed in England renting this property. You conspired to steal the

Waldemar diamond causing a deliberate house fire in which, during the confusion and panic, you intended to steal the jewel casket kept ready on the dressing table on the day she was set to visit Buckingham Palace for an audience with the Queen. Only you were both foiled, for unbeknown to either of you, the Grand Duchess, on hearing a fire had broken out, suspecting mischief, instructed the precious gem be placed in one of the teapot collectables, to be hidden in the garden by the faithful retainer, Molteno. The problem being, the old fellow had grown doddery, absent-minded and forgot where he had put it. Only now has this clever girl managed to locate the jewel."

"Actually," said Betty modestly, Police Steam Man clanking up the drive with his mobile support unit, a wagon carrying coal and a tank of water, and P.C Johns on his bicycle, the H.Q. being telephoned earlier, "an acorn distracted me and a gormless big carp, hundreds of years old, who lives in the pond,

found it for me. All I had to do was fetch a twig."

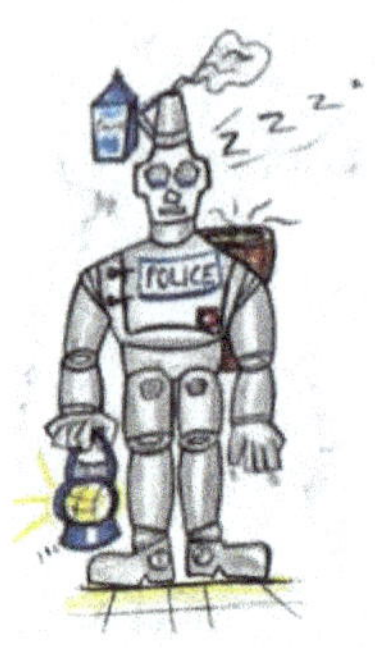

CHAPTER
9
Betty's Hero

The grease-smudged boy in overalls, stood atop of a pair of step ladders, gave the thumbs up.

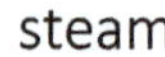

"The principle is definitely the same as general steam engines of all types," pontificated the village constable, tightening a final bolt with a spanner. "Now, Lucian, is that coal all loaded?"

"Yep."

"Good, then I'll set flame to the kindling. We'd better stand back. If the shed burns down, no worry," he laughed, striking a  vesta, then waving the match about the screwed-up balls of newspaper and bits of wood. "It will take a while to build up enough pressure, then we'll see what this thing is capable of."

"Oh, do look," whimpered Winnie White, warming her mittens by the rising heat, the metal rivets rumbling and rattling. "Our friend's eyes are starting to glow. Isn't he cute."

Zmunxy was so enthralled she wanted to hug the contraption.

The police steam man had become an official part of the local force, his first outing was a disaster – but with certain modifications his latest trials proved successful, its beat being to patrol up and down the village High Street, and this, with a slight tweaking of a gear lever, he could just about manage.

Automatically straight down one side of the pavement, stop, cross the road and patrol up the other side, and repeat the same.

The oily smoke was, at times, a bother, but burning coal in the 'clip-on' fire basket was welcomed by passers by going in and out of shops who, in this wintry weather, were most agreeably able to warm themselves by the mobile brazier.

A greater police presence was thus established, and the fact it was a machine man fascinated the local papers who wrote him up on the front pages...

Glim Glumswick ECHO

Parochial council presses for increased police presence along High Street in country village – trials begin.

What the readers say:

MR KEMPTON OF OLD PASTURE LANE: *'One gets used to it. At first I found the noise, the clanking of metal parts as it plods along, quite annoying, The smell of coal, plumes of smoke funnelled from the tip of his head. But the police must do something to cope with the increase in crime by these awful boys. I notice council workmen were repairing the pavement where cracks have been appearing due to the heavy weight of the steam constable breaking paving slabs!'*

MRS PHILPOT, POSTMAN'S COTTAGE: *'The noise and smoke – troublesome, but we do appreciate his nice, warm coal fire. But my, oh my, does the police steam man look impressive! People just stop and stare. P.C. Johns sometimes walks beside him with his bicycle, and you know, I wonder if it can think. Can it?'*

Loyal to Queen and country, a patriot of the first order, Major Sefton-Dudley flew a Union Jack outside his house from a flagpole. Proud to be British, certainly proud to have served the Empire, both in the Persian campaign and out in India, when in those days much of the world map was coloured pink.

Oh, like many a retired army major before and since, he had absolutely no time for slackers, nor incompetence. For example, he had precious little patience with the established county police force, this due in part to the chief constable Sir James Felby's annoying habit of regularly beating him at golf on the local links. The police, in his mind, were both bungling and ponderous - slow off the mark. For instance, when his house on the downs got burgled, most likely the work of a certain Alfie Nibbs, the doddery old officer who attended, the village policeman at the time, was found very lacking and slow-witted.

Young Betty Zmunx, on the other hand, was gaining something of a reputation as a sleuth. He knew she was sharp, why, it was she who had saved his life by a whisker when the 'Pencil Case' poisoning concerning crushed berries of deadly nightshade had almost done for him. Thus, when a curious and intriguing family matter came to his notice, it was to Miss Medley's singularly talented niece the major decided to turn. Early, in fact on a sunny May morning, unseasonably warm, he hoisted the Jolly Roger in place of the Union flag high on the breeze. This, an agreed signal the old army man had devised

for when he required Betty's advice - his house easily in view of the Zmunx's cottage further down. Betty, drawing back her curtains that Saturday morning, peering out of her loft window, her bedroom situated beneath  the sweet-scented thatch, caught sight of the black-and-white pirate's ensign fluttering on the breeze from the tall flagpole on Major Dudley's front lawn, as indeed did Aunt Medley, already up and about laying the table for breakfast, ham and eggs sizzling in the pan.

***

"Found this walrus-hide portmanteau belonging to my late elder brother, Colonel Loughton Dudley, up in the attic," said the Major. "Haven't ventured up there for years. Set of diaries, journals, assorted ephemera and, in particular, lot of old silver-plate. Must be quite valuable, s'pose, just don't know where to put the lot. Me glass cabinets are full of me medals and war memorabilia. What should I do, Betty? Donate the lot to the vicar's roof fund - might make a few quid, yer never know. I've gort enough ruddy silver meself, just no room for Loughton's stuff, see. Shame to keep it up in the attic, though. I'm keen to hear your views, young lady. You're a rum kid, value your opinion, wot."

An idea sprang into the girl's head. A strong possibility arose. Loughton Dudley's silver, *or maybe, perchance*, somebody else's, she wondered.

"Have you taken on anyone recently, Major?" Furrowing her brow, her eyes were shrewdly assessing the old soldier, who Aunt Medley had once been romantically linked with as an item! Erroneously, of course.

"Martley, good chappie," came the clipped response. "Ex-army does for my general factotum - odd-job fella. His wife cooks and cleans - since Mrs Laker my domestic retired."

Betty doggedly persisted. "References?"

"'Scuse me," a woman with a shrill voice interrupted. "Shall I bring in the tea, Major, elevenses, like? Hot buttered scones, nice damson jam, pot of clotted cream."

A prim, skinny domestic dressed in starched uniform, aged in her late forties eyed Betty in a condescending manner, screwing her nose up. She'd popped her head round the door. The timing proved worrying. Had she been listening, keeping her eye to the keyhole, as it were?

Eavesdropping? The girl certainly hoped not. On

reflection, her questioning of the major had been a tad abrupt - officious, similar to an examining magistrate.

"Splendid, Mrs Martley. Lay for two. Betty will be staying, won't you my dear? Two cups an' saucers."

"Rather," said the girl, gleefully.

Who could resist such a spread, after all. But the domestic looked ill-at-ease, her expression was not the companionable one of a friendly servant.

Striking a vesta and lighting his bulldog pipe, blowing wreaths of blue smoke from the corner of his mouth, Major Dudley was quick to make small talk of the proposed police mobile unit that received recent publicity, not all of it positive. The major, an ex-army man, was scathing.

"Pair of carts - wagons drawn by worn-out nags. How in blazes name are this old fire pump and the one carrying stocks of coal meant to keep pace with a mechanical steam patrolman - absurd," he chuckled, having, like other folk, warmed his hands gratefully from the metal officer's fire basket during the winter while shopping along the village High Street.

"Whereabouts is that old silver? Your brother Loughton's, I mean," the girl enquired after a decent interval, tucking into her second scone.

"Up in the attic. Told ya - portmanteau, never mentioned it to anyone else, of course. Personal family doings. Come'n, Betty, get that third scone down ya. Dollop the cream on thick."

Martley, the general factotum, was summoned by the major into the sitting room a half hour later, being requested to give the girl a lift into the village on the horse and trap.

"Going that way anyhow, sir," he answered smugly, buttoning his waistcoat. "Pick up a supply of pig manure, sacks from the ironmongers - be a pleasure."

He seemed personable enough - muscular and fit, clean shaven, smartly turned out. He wore a collarless shirt and the nape of his neck revealed something alarming. Not a birth mark, but pink calamine lotion applied to a scorch, a burn - the back of his left hand likewise blemished.

***

"Now, young lady, up you go," Martley grinned. Clear of the half-timbered house. Hurrying her across the drive to the waiting carriage, he assisted Zmunxy clamber up onto the box seat. Why, the fellow seemed civil enough. Although, truth be told, in her mind was deep speculation. How exactly had those burns got there? A domestic accident? Hardly likely. You see, she had herself been in close proximity to police steam man, the metal parts grew very hot to touch - exceedingly so. His mechanical hands, 'grabbers' as P.C. Johns called them, warmed up quick. Considering that robbery of Sir Winton Clarke's silver hadn't the papers mentioned the police steam man grappled with the miscreant when all of a sudden, the water evaporated in his tank causing malfunction. Burnt up his coal.

"What a lovely day, 'scuse me askin', are you the niece of Major Dudley? Related?"

"No," she replied. The trap jogged along, drawn by a chestnut mare. "Major Dudley is acquainted with my aunt. They attend church regularly."

"I see. Atten' meself. Christmas and Easter mostly." He cracked the whip on the horse's broad flank causing the mare to gain pace. He cracked the whip harder, now the horse was positively galloping along the lane.

"Oh, we are going a bit fast. Mighn't we slow down?" Miss Zmunx said, not liking the turn of events one bit. She experienced a sudden surge of fear as hedgerow trees and telegraph poles whizzed past. "You're taking the long way round to the village."

She had a sick, queer feeling in the pit of her stomach. "We're coming up to the dip. Reign in, why don't you?" she cried.

"Now, miss," he shouted back, relishing the speed, the fact she was growing scared. "What woz you gassing about to the Major. Mention of some old portmanteau. Wife heard talk of valuable silver."

"Yes, it's you isn't it, Mr Martley? You're the thief who stole the squire's silver. You hid it up in the attic. Only by chance Major Dudley was going through his brother's things."

Down the slope, the trap rattling at a frightening pace, the wheels spinning faster and faster, Betty could barely hold on, the carriage frame was vibrating so much. Suddenly, without warning, Martley leaned over and jumped, rolling onto the grassy bank. He got up, brushed himself down and gloated, watching the out-of- control horse and trap hurtling to disaster. For, as he planned, an abrupt turn was approaching in the country lane. The carriage would overturn and smash into the trees. He was alright course he was with the fields and the downland view.

"You little snitch," he cried with a bland rudeness. "Trying to part me from my swag, woz ya? This'll teach you to meddle. Going to grass on me, tell the coppers. Oh, you woz warm, very close, but the wife saw through your little game. You ain't so clever clogs n'more."

'This is it,' were Betty's last thoughts. 'I'm going to end up a ghost.' She squeezed her eyes shut. The galloping horse kicking up clouds of dust, wild eyed and whinnying. The coming smash, the dizzy tumbling of the carriage as it struck the corner and rolled over.

Then, out of nowhere, came a noisy scraping of iron-shod feet. A familiar clunk - hssssh - clunk, hssssh - a noise she knew well. Might she yet have a chance? Twisting round, she was gratified to see POLICE STEAM MAN rapidly gaining, stomping along under blue skies, with his fire basket ablaze, flames dancing behind his slit eyes, gushing coal smoke into the air from his chimney helmet. P.S.M.'s arm swung out, great metal hands, or 'grabbers' as they were called, clamped to the backboard of the runaway carriage, his metal feet scraping the surface of the road in a shower of sparks. Thus, horse and trap alike were forced to reduce speed, gently coming to rest

over by the verge. A carriage accident, or rather a cowardly act of murder, averted.

Betty clung to the box seat crying in relief. Meanwhile, a drooping saucepan head allowed emission of compressed air, alas, the metal officer had literally run out of steam.

"Phew, that was lucky, Betty," said P.C. Johns, having parked his bicycle further along, making an arrest handcuffing Martley whom he had bopped on the head with his truncheon, trying to do a runner across the field but getting his gaiters snared in the wire fence. "The Major's odd-job man, isn't he? Bloomin' reckless."

Betty managed to smile, dabbing her watery eyes with a hanky - shocked, but recovering. "That man stole Sir Winton Clarke's silver; he was the nearly-nabbed thief over at Wormley Stowe. The silver ornaments are up in Major Dudley's attic, stuffed in a portmanteau."

"Excellent, I shall get along there presently. Y'know," the P.C. said with a smirk, "steam man went barmy. For some reason, after lunch, my officer decides to walk onto the downs. Well, he's like a motorcar in certain respects, runs well, but only has limited fuel. I do hope the H.Q. Committee approve the support unit, it'll make my job that much easier. As it is, we'll have all the bother of getting the wagonette up here and winching his bulk into the back so I can take him home to the police house. That'll cost a fair penny, charged to Wellingford C.I.D. Haddock won't appreciate that one bit."

***

Kindling in place, police steam man's fire basket was ignited, and in no time, steam raised, Westinghouse air brakes tested, oil applied – the metal contraption was pointed in the direction of

Wormley Stowe and off he went. Now, we must address the thorny issue of 'can a mechanical man actually think ... appraise a situation, act for itself'.

"By Gad," Inspector Haddock later confided, "bizarre as it seems, how else did P.S.M. know the right route, judge the speed required to catch up, enabled to hop over obstructions such as boundary walls and farm gates?"

Truth be known, he very nearly pulled off a smart arrest. Except for one unfortunate factor – about to seize the crook by the scruff of his neck, P.S.M. shuddered to a standstill. Steam and smoke from his chimney helmet rapidly thinning to nil emissions. The same problem arose in the case of Edwina Marples who caught sight of a trespasser in her garden. The miscreant ran off, police steam man gave chase but, alas, mechanically seized up. Only. one conclusion may be drawn: the coal in his firebox burnt off too rapidly, steam pressure could not be maintained over the longer distance. In conclusion, the C.I.D. department at Wellingford H.Q., under Haddock, proposed *a mobile support unit* should be formed without delay, a rapid response unit able to cope with supplying additional coal and water when the need arose. Henceforth, a horse-drawn ex-fire pump and a cart were requisitioned. The cross-country chases could now be sustained – criminals on the run beware!

Trials began in earnest – children did not just have steam police man to wave at but could follow the mobile support unit being put through its paces over in a field behind the Mitre Inn. The unit eventually being housed not too far from the police house in a disused stable block.

CHAPTER

10

Wormly Halt

Sat in the compartment at the back of a two-coach train, Betty Zmunx could overhear the guard and porters as they made last minute preparations for departure at eleven o'clock.

"Beg pardon, Mr Fraser, zir, but there's a corfin bound for Creesdale. I'll bring it up from the parcels office on the station trolley."

Her best friend, Lizzie Meredith, sat opposite on the cloth-covered seat.

"Oh, Betty, we'll have such jolly fun at the department store, and lunch in the restaurant on the third floor." The girls were jubilant on their day out.

"Got me the flower, fish and poultry boxes,"

droned a man's voice. "Bags of seed potatoes, mail sack and baskets of plums," said the guard standing by to assist loading the elm coffin mostly covered in canvas, presumably for protecting the wood finish.

The branch did occasionally transport coffins along the line and it was normal. "Not too 'eavy, zen."

"Aye, not like the last one; some big fat bloke. Murder it were, nearly did me back in."

Betty and Lizzie couldn't help giggling, poking their heads out of the compartment window.

The stationary train was due out in five minutes. The sunny platform was alive with sparkling rainbow patterns, the station bedecked with colourful flower tubs, hanging baskets and window boxes, the smell of sooty smoke wafting down the train from the huffing locomotive up front.

"Right, that's that, Mr Fraser, blow your whistle, wave the green flag and you're off, corfin stowed allus right."

"No bother."

Doors slammed, the engine tooted its whistle, echoing about the station precincts, and couplings clanked as the train moved steadily out of the country station.

The girls talked excitedly to one another. "*The four points* are these," said Lizzie, passing her bag of pineapple chunks. "One... Grandma Nibbs

uses a witch hazel broomstick, two... she owns a big, black cat, three... she makes potions up into bottles, four... she's ugly and has a hairy top lip and warts on her chin."

"The grandmother absolutely hates the fat policeman. Golly, you know she may have cast another of those horrid spells, that's why he's getting all these bicycle punctures, flat tyres at the drop of a hat; the last one forced him to walk for miles

between villages. My Aunt Medley thinks he needs a new bike, but we know different.”

Talk drifted to purchasing new bonnets and the latest Miss Bradden pot boiler which they both liked lots. The rustic charm of a branch line station cannot be denied. At the next stop, Wormley halt, the train rattled to a standstill.

The porter at these halts had plenty of time to darn his socks, cook meals and work on his flower and vegetable plots. Here, amid the twittering birdsong and gentle hissing of the engine, an interesting altercation took place.

The coffin; I ain’t travelling in the guard’s van n’more with that thing,” he said, shakily. “It’s alive, summat’s alive in there. I ’eard long fingernails scratching the underneath of the lid. Ghastly, the smell of decay is everywhere. Something that’s alive, but not ...”

The guard was evidently sorely perplexed and had summoned the porter to his assistance.

"*A living dead.* I catch your drift, Mr Fraser. Did it bite you with its fangs? There's blood on yer shirt collar, man!"

"Naw, that were from cutting meself shaving. But, honestly, Mr Tempest - sounded like long, calcified fingernails, blinkin' talons, scratching against the lid. I'm fair petrified after travelling in the guard's van all alone. The dead has come alive, that coffin h'aint right."

By now, Betty and her friend Lizzie had got out of

the compartment, stood in the sunshine listening to unfolding events.

"Best if we get young Lidden, my junior porter, to run into the village for a priest. Isn't that the correct procedure? *A vampire* is what we got 'ere, guvnor," said the porter anxiously.

"Might I take a look? Only a peep," asked Betty curiously, not very impressed by the lack of nerve.

"Wha', you, a girl?" exclaimed the guard.

"I might just be able to solve the puzzle. I'm rather good at that sort of thing, as Lizzie here will tell you."

Without asking permission, the girl clambered up into the van, fearless of *'the undead'*, more concerned to get to the heart of the matter. Vampires, she realised from basic reading of girls' adventure annuals, only ever came out at night, after all.

Clues were forthcoming. When she pulled across the canvas sheet, she was amazed to spot tiny air holes bored into the elm lid. What's more, the lid was loosely held in place, hinged along one side. By now, the porter joined her, helping to lift the lid. The waft of liquid manure, the pungent, acrid stench in the guard's van was intense, providing a further clue.

As the lid creaked open, Betty and Mr Tempest were confronted by a dumpy black and tan sow resting lazily on its side on a soiled bed of straw. The pig snorted and belched before, unbothered, it went

back to sleep, *five little pigs* nestling at its stomach teats.

"Well, I never!" exclaimed the porter, scratching his beard.

The porter continued, "The village wheelwright, carpenter Joe Osmond at Glim Glumswick, acts as the undertaker. He also part owns a smallholding out at Creesdale, a pig farm. This fellow must have utilised one of his spare coffins to transport the sow and her offspring. She were fed a mash of bottled beer and barley oats to keep her sedated for the railway journey up the line. I'll not write out a complaint chit on this occasion, but when I next see him at the Mitre Inn, I'll be bound to have words. Carry on here, Mr Fraser, this girl is to be commended. Your name please, young lady?"

"Betty Zmunx."

After shopping in town, making the return journey along the branch, the girls, laden down with packages, strolled happily back to the village. The sun was still up and it was boiling hot. Along Old Pasture Lane they met the fat policeman looking very despondent; he was pushing a brand new bicycle, waddling along.

"It's no good," he gasped, flushed red and sweating profusely. "I'm still getting punctures, that's three today already. Why me, what have I done to deserve this?"

"Your bicycle clips. Take them off at once," cried Betty, realising at last what others could not. "You see, Mr Johns, what accompanies you when you're out riding?"

"Yes, by jingo, my cycle clips. I've worn these for years."

The fat policeman, at Betty's specific direction, let her examine the inside of each springy metal ring. Strange symbols, *runes* they were called, magical diagrams, had been scratched with the point of a sharp instrument, creating ill luck to the wearer. Grandma Nibbs had been responsible - she was sure of it.

CHAPTER

11

Aunt Medley, Edwina Zmunx and Betty were sat around the table in the parlour about to start tea when Mrs Zmunx exclaimed in surprise, "Who burnt my saucepan? It's got a hole in the bottom. I came back from the shops, and there it was on the range. I remember quite clearly washing it up in soft soap at lunchtime after boiling some milk; it was spick and span, good and shiny."

"Well, dearest," said Aunt Medley, choosing a cucumber sandwich, meticulously putting it upon her plate. "Betty's been at school, and I have been at Glim Glumswick doing flowers for the church. I got back *after* you." Both women scrutinised the schoolgirl suspiciously.

"Don't look at me so, please," said Betty. "It's not my fault, it's really not. I can see the daft old saucepan from here. It's burnt black, but not by me."

"Then who was it burnt the saucepan if none of us?"

Betty decided that after tea, before doing her homework for her teacher Miss Tern at the schoolhouse, she would look more closely into this mystery to put mother's mind at rest. A risible enough puzzle, but a puzzle just the same. Aunt Medley was going out into the garden to clear the bird table of any remaining scraps which at night tended to attract four-legged scavengers such as foxes, stoats and weasels ... or rats.

Thus, Betty aged six, after buttoning up her winter coat, allowing her aunt to fuss over her woolly hat - snatched from the peg - and mittens from her coat pocket, went out into the garden. The snow lay settled, the low temperature keeping the surface, the crust, hard and firm. Together they went up the path which had received a scattering of coal fire cinders that had been collected in a bucket. Even from the glow of the storm lantern, the perceptive girl saw quite clearly a rogue set of footprints leading across the lawn.

"Odd."

"What's odd, dear?"

"Nothing much, Auntie."

However, young Miss Zmunx's sharp eye realised quickly that one footprint was more deeply embedded than the other - more weight applied on the foot. The footprints leading away in the snow were different: one had a chunky sole, the other more like a shoe, the tread a lighter pattern. In plain words, *odd shoes, not a pair.* Well, who normally wears different shoes to walk about?

Whilst her aunt tidied the bird table, the girl - using her bicycle lamp for light - traced the oddly matching footprints over to a flowerbed behind which was a wild bracken hedge that ran beside Prudie Lane. Someone, even an animal perhaps, had recently created a ragged gap roughly parting the foliage, bending and snapping twigs.

"Do come on, dear, it's far too cold to be hanging about. Botheration, where are you? What on earth are you up to now? Betty, answer me, don't dither."

"Coming," Betty said obediently, trudging over the snowy lawn, clasping her aunt's hand in hers and walking back to the house. The bright, hissing glow of the hurricane lamp warmed her cheeks, yet a far warmer glow filled her from within, for she was that little bit nearer to solving the saucepan mystery and, more importantly, growing more confident in her ability to search out clues.

Next morning at breakfast, Betty happily ate her boiled egg and toast soldiers, but her mother was still perplexed about the burnt saucepan and would go on. "Leaving the pan on the hob to boil too long. Forgetful. Boiling potatoes. You see, the heat and soot blackening the outside. Water evaporates, causing damage to the base."

"Well," said Aunt Medley, full of admiration, "Betty has solved the mystery, haven't you, dear? You told me while I was applying tooth powder upstairs."

"Why, I believe it was Betty who burnt my saucepan," accused Mrs Zmunx, pouring out more tea for everybody. "You can't pull the wool over my eyes, dear."

"Mother, really, it is no use blaming me, it's Mr Stumpy who's responsible."

"The gypsy over at the encampment?" Edwina Zmunx frowned, feeling at a complete loss.

"Mended a chair leg for you, sat on the kitchen step smoking his clay pipe. You gave him sixpence. Last week, let him come in and warm himself."

"I did, too, but what does that grimy, smelly old man have to do with my saucepan?"

"When having his mug of tea that Saturday, Mother,

he must have glimpsed your pan boiling on the hob and taken quite a liking to it. They are both the same shape and size, after all."

"Tell your mama how it was done. Don't shilly-shally," insisted Aunt Medley, cutting up her bacon.

The six year old, dipping her toast soldier into the orange egg yolk, took a delicious bite before continuing. "The footsteps in the snow. You see, Mr Stumpy wanted to hide his wooden leg, so he would not be suspected. He slipped an India-rubber wellington over the timber toe and came across from the caravans after he saw you hurrying down the lane to the village shops. He came across with his old, filthy, burnt saucepan wanting to replace his useless, horrid one with your nice clean one - and he did.

Mr Stumpy unlatched the back door and got in that way after cutting across the garden."

CHAPTER
12
Tunnel Vision

That Sunday morning after church, during sherry at the vicarage, being October, the editor of the parish magazine, Humphrey Searles, had approached Aunt Medley asking if she could contribute a short piece on local ghosts - Edwina Zmunx, Betty's mother, having already written a humorous golfing anecdote - fit for the Christmas number to be published in December.

Aunt Medley agreed but was cautious what ghost should feature. Jill's Tea Rooms, purportedly haunted by a ghostly knocking, put down to water pipes. The Mitre Inn possessed a haunted four-poster bed; *doubtful*, of course. Old country folklore legends abounded, but it soon became clear, after diligent enquiry, that Kerry, the female gravedigger, and Mr Nincolme Poopson, with his already documented case of his departed pet, Beezer, the spectral hound, were the best sources for village ghosts.

The day blowy and overcast, Mr Poopson had been returning a repaired bicycle to Reg Greenway, stopping off at the tobacconist, when Aunt Medley, shopping with her niece, Betty, waved him over. She explained about the church magazine article and the signalman's first impulse was to be different, be daring.

"Why bovver wiv boring ol' ghosts? Y'know, blinkin' headless grey ladies in castles, sheeted spectres in manor 'ouses, skellintons in the boneyard, movin' ashtrays. I fink I gort summink far more h'oringinal. Effer heard of *the ghost train*?" He paused to lick his lips. "No, you neffer, I'd bet, Miss Medley, but I 'ave. I seen it, see. Swear orn me ol' grandmuvver's grave. I seed the ghost train, I 'ave. Corst yer though!"

"How much, Mr Poopson?" asked Betty clutching Aunt's hand, thinking he had a cheek.

"A shillin' each. Penny fer you young uns, for all yer witnesses wot aufenticates like, one shillin'. Now, you got yersel' an article wurf readin', aint yer?"

The aunt had to admit parishioners might be interested in the ghost train, but she must tread carefully. "But people do so like their traditional ghosts, Mr Poopson. There's a quaint charm associated with the clanking of a suit of armour at midnight, rattling chains at the dead of night, queer glowing lights in the hedgerow, candles blown out, the headless grey lady."

"Lot of ol' baloney. If it's the genuine fing you're arter, *the ghost train* wins by a furlong. So 'appens the anniversary's tomorra night. Yuzz, night o' the full moon."

"Anniversary!" exclaimed the aunt. "What anniversary?"

"The crash in Churnly Tunnel. The tunnel collision; people killed, o' course, ooh 1868, the Copperknobs runnin' the show then."

"Copperknobs?"

"Type of locomotive, ma'am. H'engineerin' marvels, they wuzz'; big, tall stacks, steam boiler, tender, open carriages, lot o' wood involved. Lot o' deffs."

"So this Copperknob returns?" asked the girl.

"Not from the grave, Betty, from the tunnel marrf, see. Ooh, a terrible smash it were. I won't go into details; long afore our time, o' course. Long afore GN&SR engines of today.

"You know, I'd quite like to take you up on your offer, Mr Poopson. Betty, I'm sure, backs my decision. The article I'm writing would be original, offer a new slant, but the ghost train had better be genuine."

better be genuine."

Mr Poopson nodded. "Genuine as could be. Meet me tomorra nigh' wiv yer witnesses, shillin' apiece, Glim

Glumswick signal box, 9 p.m. Got that, ladies? Bottom o' steps."

Aunt Medley and Betty managed to gather more than thirty interested parties, locals prepared to fork out a shilling for the privilege of witnessing *the ghost train* for themselves. The vicar, his wife, Mrs Bunn from next door, Betty's best chums Winnie White and Lizzie were amongst the folk who, at the allotted hour, congregated at the foot of the signal box on a dark and chilly evening in October, hurricane lamps hissing, oil lanterns aglow.

"Are we headed for the tunnel?" enquired Betty's mother, wrapped up well against the light drizzle then falling, fully expectant of a long, damp trudge up the tracks to the sooty tunnel mouth, and a freezing long wait gleaning zilch!

"Naw," answered Mr Nincolme Poopson emphatically, "The crossing gates is where we is most likely to see the ghost train. Now, ladies and gents, I must ask you to douse yer lights, ven we shall cross the track and wait. Place yer shillin's in me saucepan as yer go."

The darkness encroached upon the little railway. Maybe there was a full moon, but this night the golden orb of mystery, watching the world since time immemorial, associated with the howling of wolves, remained concealed behind cloud cover, the drizzle continuing.

Everyone was hushed and expectant, stood in a huddle, Mr Poopson now at the fore, accessing the gated level crossing with a practised professional eye, his unlit tobacco pipe stuck in the corner of his mouth, his jaw determined. He consulted his pocket watch on the end of a big silver fob chain.

"I hear something!" exclaimed the padre.

"Did you hear what, dearest?" The vicar's wife clung to his arm, listening, peering across the tracks, seeing things where they shouldn't be.

"Quiet pleeze, yer worship," the signalman said in a hushed tone. The waiting intensified.

Everyone was thrilled to be scared, scared stiff by the unexplained, awaiting 'the summoned', the sight of a spectral machine of yore. How many souls lost their lives so hideously being burned to death in the tunnel. The Copperknob, the olden locomotive, the footplate crew presumably mangled in the wreckage, the flimsy wooden, open carriages, highly inflammable. One could but morbidly speculate, all this grim imagining contributing to the prevailing atmosphere. *An appointment with death*. The tension was palpable. Suddenly, everyone gasped, surprised out of their wits.

POLICE STEAM MAN emerged from the tunnel followed by P.C. Johns wheeling, his bicycle.

"Illegal rave."

"Eh?" said the vicar.

"Ahem, **R**ailway **A**ssembly **V**enue **E**ndangerment -

Come on everybody, orf you go now."

CHAPTER

13

Rumbled

Upon a spring morning in April, Aunt Medley unlatched the back door and brought in a cardboard grocery box full of odds and ends for the jumble sale. Faithful Mrs Appleton, the Zmunxs' domestic, bustled from outside with another box, plonking hers on the kitchen table alongside the other.

The sale was taking place over at the village hall that Saturday at ten. The Reverend Smithson, who had only recently married Miss Caterham, was encouraging everyone at church to collect whatever, thus contributing to raising money for the church roof restoration fund. A very worthy cause, because strips of lead were urgently required to stem the recent spate of leaks, thus preventing the need for rainwater collecting buckets placed beneath the brass eagle lectern and stone font.

Betty Zmunx peeped into each box, checking the selection of dingy contents on offer. A tatty china tea service, stack of picture frames, Mr Rodney's mantel clock with its back off, woollens, Mrs Lamb's old cat dish, worn dog lead and studded collar, a heap of women's periodicals, an old man's frayed coat with two buttons missing, donated by Joe Larch.

The girl went back upstairs to read her slim, little, beautiful Beatrix Potter book, biding time, for she had previously been commandeered by Aunt Medley for jumble sale service over at the village hall.

The village hall, where numerous activities took place, was built on a plot of land donated by Sir Winton Clarke. For instance, the Glim Glumswick Dramatic Society held its plays here, the productions organised by Mrs Stacey, costumes made by Miss Lloyd and Mr Fernly Frith. The players were a social distraction that, over the years, provided residents young and old with a good deal of pleasure. This morning, though, the village hall was a hive of jumbling activity.

By ten, the jumble sale was in full swing; the hall was packed, card and trestle tables heaped with old junk, and during the first hour's clamour, the hunt for bargains only intensified. Betty, who was selling ladies' hats, noticed a heated argument taking place on the stall opposite, concerned with bric-a-brac, between Mrs Rae and a gentleman wearing a shabby suit, spats and a bowler.

"Bloomin' sakes, I'se offered yer tuppence," he said sullenly. "Nows I says a shillin', woman, and yer still refuses. Blast it all, 'ere's two bob. Now 'and the dish over. I'm being generous, I am."

"Reserved - r-e-s-e-r-v-e-d," Mrs Rae emphasised, taking no nonsense from this determined jumbler. "My niece, Val, was in earlier and is to pay me a halfpenny when she comes back from the shops, walking the baby with a pram."

The man was flabbergasted and could not believe what he was hearing. "Gawd save us, woman - favouritism. I'm offering yer more, not less. What's a halfpenny to two bob for a blasted ol' dish what's cracked?"

"That dish is reserved for my niece and that's an end. You realise we have a nearly complete tea service over here; plenty of dishes in better condition than that old cat dish."

"That wuzz the one for me," he sighed, no match for the woman. "I tell you what, love, I'll take the teapot, cups and saucers. Can I get yer a cuppa over at the counter? There's not much of a queue at present. I'm gasping." The man grinned, doffing his bowler, trying on the charm and succeeding.

"I will - two sugars, ta!" Mrs Rae replied gaily. "An' a bun?"

"Certainly."

"Thought any more 'bout my offer for the cat dish?" He struck a match and lit his cigarette, glancing at her slyly.

"No, I'll pack up the tea service for you in this newspaper. You just get on and fetch me my tea."

The gentleman in the spats and bowler ambled across the hall to the kitchen cubbyhole, the refreshment counter where the tea urn, plates, cups and saucers, sugar bowls and cutlery were stacked.

Talking of tea, Aunt Medley's friend, Gertrude West, on 'old furniture', came hurrying over to the used hat stall - she helped with flowers at the parish church - a cup of scalding hot, fiendishly strong tea in either hand. "The armchair and sofa's gone. You know, with the chipped round table with the wobbly leg."

"Oh, I am pleased," gushed Betty's aunt, beaming from ear to ear. "How much? Did they fetch the asking price?"

"A bit below, but that'll do. Reg, my husband, will undertake delivery later this afternoon to Mr Morton's cottage on the back of his wagonette."

The girl was hardly listening, being distracted by the excitement over on the bric-a-brac stall opposite. Mrs Rae had fainted. The vicar and his wife crouched over, administering smelling salts.

The woman's eyes fluttered and she was soon on her feet, wondering what all the fuss was about, once more taking charge of her stall, while still more hordes of avid jumblers paid their admission at the door and entered the fray.

"Where's me dish?" demanded a young woman barging through a throng of jumblers sorting woollens, using her pram as a battering ram, children in tow. "Halfpenny, you promised, Ivy."

"I've got it here, Val - least did 'ave. Now, where in heaven's name could it have got to? The cat dish was over here by the old carriage clocks. I even put a reserved label on it specially."

"Excuse me," exclaimed Aunt Medley, taking time out from making a display of ladies' hats. "That man, the gentleman wearing the spats and bowler, the shabby suit?" Val wheeled her pram aside, marshalling her children to allow the aunt through.

"I know the one," exclaimed Mrs Rae. "T'was he who kindly fetched me a cup of tea. He forked out for the China service."

"I think, myself, he was very deceitful and took the opportunity of pinching the cat dish when you fainted earlier. Betty, who was watching all the while, insists he may have poisoned your tea, adding powders. She saw him taking an awfully long time lingering over spooning in sugar. He won't escape, Betty's gone after him."

"But what about my cat dish?" moaned Val.

Zmunxy was keen to identify the dish stealer watching him for definite enter the High Street antiques shop, making earnest conversation with the pompous proprietor, Mr Veriker. The manager stood behind the glass counter wearing his frock coat and a red carnation buttonhole.

The girl pushed open the door to the shop; the bell pinged. "Yes, what do you want, child? Can't you see I'm busy?"

"I'm ever so sorry, Mr Veriker, but that cat dish belongs to bric-a-brac at the jumble sale. It was reserved for Mrs Rae's niece, Valerie, to be sold for helping towards the church roof restoration fund."

The man sneered. "I ain't a-caring for what this little toady says. It's mine, I told you, I got it fair 'n' square, see, at the jumble sale orf a very nice lady, I did."

"You put something in her tea to make her dizzy and faint," said Betty, confident she was in the right and knew what she was saying.

"Stoppid, toady - lies, lies."

The manager, a fine, upstanding fellow in the community, sided with the girl.

"I refuse to hand this item back to you, sir. Am I to alert our local constabulary, P.C. Johns? Look sharp, young Mr Levenson - hat, coat and stick, m'lad. Fast as you can down to the church hall. Hup, hup." The assistant did as bidden.

"Alright, alright," said the nasty gentleman. "I'm orf, I'm art of 'ere. Why, you little toady, you." He shook his fist at the teenager, tearing across the High Street to board a bus and make a quick departure.

"My name is Betty Zmunx, actually," she cried after him, running to the door, very red in the face, indignant of his coarse and vulgar attitude.

"My dear young lady," crooned the antiques dealer, indicating his assistant should bother himself no more in the apprehension of this villainous rascal.

"Inform the vicar at once that this item is no mere cat dish, but rare Ming dynasty porcelain worth many thousands of pounds. I believe the church shall face no problems of a leaking roof in future, and much more restoration work may be done besides, including the planned extension to the village hall, the dressing room area for the stage I heard mention of from Mrs Stacey."

CHAPTER

14

Mr Tadworths Watch

The branch station, with its coal siding, was situated just outside the village, off the main Glim Glumswick to Wellingford Road, the forecourt approached along a leafy lane bordered by hedgerow trees, lit at night and early morning by a row of gas lamps. Beyond the wicker fence with tin advertisements for Lipton's and Wright's coal tar soap were the platforms. A train was in, waiting to depart.

The country station possessed a steep, gabled roof with tall, angular chimneys, the frontage timber-clad presenting mullioned windows, and at the front entrance a pair of bright, glossy brown doors adorned with big, brass doorknobs which led to the ticket hall. Along the platform, from whose awning hung a two-sided wrought-iron clock, was the station master's office, the telegraph room, a parcels office in which tickets, date punch and booking records were housed, and the waiting rooms.

"Zorry about that there Lunnon connection o' yours, zir. Step over the footbridge, this one's for Wellingford."

A gentleman wearing a frock coat and topper dashed off up the platform to catch his train, a puffing engine approaching the gated level crossing some way distant.

"Ah, good mornin', Miss Medley, an' you too, Betty. A day to beez indoor 'n by the fire, I reckon. Bit of a nip in the air. Still, compartment'll be nice and warm. No, I'se insist, allow me to take your bag. Christmas shoppin' is we?" Aunt Medley, returning the clipped tickets to her purse, nodded. "I am myself after fine French lace and crinolines, Betty, a Beeton's children's annual at Stoate's bookshop in town."

"An' ladies, you'll get allus that 'n more, no doubt. Now, I'll just shut the carriage door for ye. Departure on time, too."

The Paddington bound London express arrived at the country station in a mass of steam and sooty smoke, engulfing passengers crossing the iron footbridge to connect with the stopping service to Wellingford. Once all were on board, with a shudder of clanking couplings, the train pulled out, soon rumbling past the crossing gates and signal box.

"*The Secret Adversary* - in that book you're reading and were telling me about last evening. Who was he, dear?"

"The vicar. It was a tough puzzler. Penfold Dimkins. I worked him out only in chapter fifteen."

"I met your fat policeman, P.C. Johns, the other day. He complained of always getting cycle punctures. He had two to mend on the morning I was at the ironmongers. The pneumatic tyres of his touring bicycle are well enough pumped up properly to the correct tension then 'bang', just as he's riding along. No reason."

Betty did not say anything, but she strongly suspected Alfie Nibb's grandmother, who the Meredith twins *and she* knew to be a witch, was at the heart of this mischief. P.C. Johns had been responsible for jailing her son, the policeman never forgiven by the family, and that's a wife, grandmother and nine feral children.

While the train lazily followed the branch out of Glim Glumswick, Aunt Medley, writing with a lead pencil stub, concerned herself with doing *The Times* crossword. Betty herself, lulled by the constant clickety-clack of the two-coach train, peered out of the carriage window at the endlessly engrossing winter's scene, the backcloth of hills, the patchwork of arable fields, passing farmsteads, thatched cob cottages with smoking chimney pots, a red-brick inn, muddy lane bordered by hedgerow trees winding along beside the track.

At the next station, a cluster of Christmas trees was quickly unloaded from the guard's van. The porter hurried into the ticket hall, barely squeezing past the booth. Several metal churns waited on the platform to be put on board, fresh milk being sent to the town of Wellingford.

Betty saw it all from the train window. She knew the stopping service regularly carried, besides passengers, fruit and vegetables in season, calves, horses, bundles of newspapers, day-old chicks and all manner of goods, serving the country villages along the line.

The girl continued to watch the activity, her sharp curiosity missing nothing. While the train remained stationary, a friendly old gentleman, known well to the Zmunxs, made an appearance, entering the compartment, doffing his tweed cap and taking a seat. Suddenly, he became very beetroot-faced and flustered.

"Why, Mr Tadworth, what a pleasure!"

"No it ain't, Miss Medley," said he, frantically searching his waistcoat. "I gorn lost my pocket watch. Oh lor', what a bind. Now where could it 'ave gone to?"

"I think one of the pointy fir trees snatched it," said Betty excitedly.

"My dear child, the watch is a solid gold repeater wot belonged to my grandpa. This be no sort of joke, y'know. Sentimental I is about that watch, very valuable an' all."

"Mr Tadworth, when I was looking out of the window, I saw you come out of the ticket hall and brush past the porter bundled with a lot of Christmas trees. You know how springy and prickly the branches are. You must have caught yourself, the branches brushed against your waistcoat while the porter squeezed past, snaring your not properly fastened fob chain, yanking the watch out. Hurry, hurry, do call out before the train leaves!"

"Well, I must say, either Betty is being terribly clever, or very, very naughty," proposed Aunt Medley, frowning in a bemused way at the kindly old gentleman sat next to her, but Mr Tadworth, not slow to take the initiative, slammed down the compartment window, tugging at the leather strap, yelling at the top of his voice, "Evans, Evans, 'fore you blow that whistle, my lad, check somethin' for me, could you? There's a shillin' for your trouble."

"Three minutes before the train departs, Mr Tadworth. What is it you want, sir?"

"Check them batch of Christmas trees in the ticket hall waiting for the delivery cart. Me fob watch mighta gort tangled, see."

Sure enough, moments later the porter came bounding up clutching in his outstretched hand the said item.

"By 'Enry, like a Yuletide bauble it were, sir ... and now I'll take that shillin' off yer if I may."

CHAPTER

15

Turf Wars

That dull morning of mist, Kerry Martlett, the female gravedigger at the parish church, after collecting her spade and a plank from the shed, despite the murky visibility for the first time, facing the church, was confronted by a most unseasonable peculiarity.

The ancient Saxon tower was infested by a growth of ripening pumpkins nurtured by unbelievably tall and sturdy vines that spread like tentacles around the stonework from base to buttress. To a keen veg grower like Kerry, with a respectable patch in her own garden, this profusion of pumpkins was somewhat at odds with mother nature, for it was now only June yet clumps of these big gourds were strangling the church tower - Absurd? Oh, they were real alright, not an imagined figment borne of the morning mist. Rubbing her chin, she wondered whether the vicar, the Rev Smithson, or his wife, might have seen this horticultural apparition from the breakfast room over at the rectory.

Putting aside her bewilderment, Kerry moseyed over to complete the new grave she was digging, ambling past a fairly recently turfed-over mound, the plot awaiting in time, a proper headstone a temporary wooden cross staked in place.

***

"Oh, what now? What's it stopped for?" asked the village constable, exasperated. "Nothing mechanical, surely? Time is getting on."

"Levers notched up into the correct position." Lucian Finn, kitted out in his work overalls, was giving everything another check. "Caps turned anticlockwise, regulator's fine, plenty of coal in the basket, so why isn't it moving?"

A squeak of metal and clattering of ball bearings heralded the steam man's saucepan head to turn and appraise the nearby corner property. One of the

metal patrolman's heavy arms hoisted, it's right clenched hand, or 'grabber', pointing over a brick wall at a lawn, on which was a yellow painted gypsy caravan with ornamental carved shutters and steps.

The house itself, Lucian recalled, belonged to a Mr Tebbit and his wife, Joyce. A retiring couple.

"Come on, come on," said an infuriated P.C.

Johns, anxious to get going, reaching up on tiptoe to rap hard on steam man's broad shoulder-pad with his bicycle pump, doing his best to avoid the inevitable coal smuts.

This impatient gesture was not appreciated by police steam man. A loud, prolonged hoot issued from a valve. Suddenly, his arm solidly pointing at the yellow caravan, clattered by his side. Hooray, he was off again, stomping one iron-shod foot in front of the other, forward motion achieved.

***

Wearing a shadeful, round parson's hat, in combination with black cassock and shiny patent shoes, the Rev Smithson looked beseechingly at his long-standing church warden. "What are we to make of it?"

He and the vicar had shared many trials and tribulations concerning the leaky, lead church roof, but this was exceptional.

"Never seen anything quite the like of," the other sighed. He looked stealthily round. Betty and her best friends Winnie White and Lizzie Meredith, the cottager Mr Tree and his portly spouse Cath, Mrs Bunn, Peg Denton and the old gossips Prissy Lloyd and Mags Gray were poised over by the roped off section of path.

"What's extraordinary are the vines, more akin to jungle foliage," mused the cleric, fumbling for his bag of jellybeans.

"Quite right. I am at a complete loss," the church warden, shielded his eyes from the sun. "charming old church, can't have it overrun by pumpkins."

The sexton, his rugged bewhiskered face bronze as a nut, strolled across, from cutting grass. "If it weren't for the possibility of structural damage, Vicar, caused by the burden of foliage clinging to the stonework, I'd happily leave 'em where they are. Folk finds the pumpkins amusing."

"What a task. Job of work, though, tackling that lot. Are Kerry and you up to it, Mr Broley? Tall ladders offer a foothold I suppose."

"Well, we'll give it a try. I'll test the lower vines with a saw. Kerry tol' me a queer sap come out of the bark when she used a penknife to make an exploratory cut, stung her fingers."

"Oh, dear," exclaimed the vicar, "Mightn't the fire brigade assist? Make an assault of the tower with axes."

"A grand idea," said the

church warden, glad of a way forward. Of course, he knew the vicar to be a clever chap anyhow, well able to deal with a crisis. The

group of villagers were dispersing.

"Betty," said Winnie, wide-eyed, "I think our pumpkins make the church tower look like it's covered in sweets."

"The whole thing's potty," offered Lizzie, sucking on a sherbet dip from Mrs Staple's sweet shop, always a stop-off point on the way home from the schoolhouse.

***

Earlier Miss Betty had wandered across to a relatively recent turfed-over hump, a few withered wreaths scattered about. The wooden cross marking the spot she knew to be temporary, this specific grave awaiting a proper cemented headstone. The roughly carved name on the cross, however, was known to her and her friends.

Grandma Nibbs

She recalled the funeral some months back - *Grandma*

Nibbs, before her death, a long-time resident of Glim Glumswick, had a notorious reputation for being a witch.

Wary of the patches of square-cut turf, a grey squirrel scampered across Betty's path.

That evening, over a mug of tea and a slice of Aunt Medley's apple pie, a flushed Lucian Finn in-between munching and slurping, much to Betty's delight proceeded to outline the events of the morning in which police steam man ground to a halt and kept pointing over the wall at the yellow painted gypsy caravan.

"P.C. Johns and I just couldn't get him to budge. He was due on patrol, see - you know, up the High Street. Well, you've accompanied him  yourself, Betty. Once the lever's notched into its groove, off he jolly well goes."

"Oh, I know he can communicate - certain he can."

"The way you lot natter on about this silly heap of junk, you'd think it real, or something. You both seem to me to talk of steam wotsit as a person.

You're fantasizing again, the realms of picture books for three-to-five-year-olds. This thing, from what I've read in the *Echo*, is one down from a mamod steam engine, way down in fact. Ask yourselves, did the engineer at the loco shed do the right thing in spending works' time and tools building a useless contraption."

"But P.S.M.'s not useless, don't you see? Mr Bunberry and Mr Gilbert were inventors who undertook to provide our local policeman with backup for his efforts to bring the crime wave down in Glim Glumswick," Spoke up Betty.

Aunt Medley poured more tea from the pot and shook her head. "How can your clanking great hulk of metal go into, say, a house, or a bank, to arrest somebody? He weighs a ton. The place would be demolished. No, I'm sorry, this P.S.M on legs is walking scrap."

Auntie's short memory, tut tut, how soon we forget - that during the giant hogweed crisis P.S.M saved the day – he was a hero!

Lucian, over his second slice of pie, suggested Betty and he take their little dogs for walkies. Why was the metal officer pointing with such determination at the yellow gypsy caravan?

Once the girl's Scotch terrier was safely on his lead, off they went leaving Aunt Medley to do the washing up.

Starting to get dark, by the time Lucian and Betty arrived at the house on the corner, tying their beloved pooches to a gatepost, the pair sneaked along by the wall, peering over to find Mrs Tebbit, Mr Tebbit's wife minding her head, as she came out of the door of the little caravan shutting it carefully behind her, clutching a duster and tin of wax polish to her bosom, thereafter as darkness swiftly settled over the garden, her figure seen vaguely mounting up a steep flight of steps to the house proper, calling "Kitty, Kitty." A smaller shape with gleaming emerald eyes leapt up, joining her at the top step, nuzzling against her leg. A light came on in the hall, then she and her cat vanished.

The coast was clear, the gypsy caravan had always fascinated Lucian Finn, now was their chance. Creeping across the lawn the little steps loomed ahead.

The caravan door possessed a latch, but with only a gentle push, not even a squeal or creak, once inside, came the real fun. Betty leaned over her friend as he took a lamp from his pocket and for a few moments a bright effusion lit up the space, and in that few seconds before the bulb failed both teenagers had to stifle their screams. An urn in the shape of a Grecian vase with a pair of deeply red glowing eyes and a tiny murmuring mouth was appraising them from the top of a writing desk – a number of sharpened pencils rolled across the blotter, there was a bookcase along one wall making up the furniture.

"Let's get out of here," cried Lucian Finn.

"One moment," A murky, vaporous shape silently shifted along the bench. "My name is Clifford Tebbit. This was once a writer's hut - my refuge. Now, I repose here. Kindly approach the bookcase, take down the hardback third from the end - top row. That is all I have to say. Good luck."

Lucian did as bidden and, without looking back, they hurried away, eager to join their pets, the book was not heavy and fairly slim.

***

Saturday morning, after breakfast, Zmunxy, gathering her chimney-pot hat and cloak, headed out to the village library - on her way, she stopped to peer through the quaintly thatched lychgate at the old church, clumps of pumpkins still smothering the Saxon tower. Yet, as is human nature, the local folk were getting used to it. The pumpkin outbreak, treated as a normal part of the scene. Although,

rightly, the vicar was determined to bring in the fire

brigade, he regarded the orange gourds as both heathen and unsightly, more appropriate for the autumnal season of ploughing and harvesting.

Betty clutched her book *Ley Lines & The Rise of Witchcraft in the County* by a certain Clifford Tebbit even tighter.

Walking up the library steps to the entrance, Betty fortuitously bumped into Professor Lallington bearing a shopping bag full of returns.

"My dear Betty, what a pleasure. Your mother and Aunt Medley keep well, I trust? My housekeeper, Mrs Hurdlestone, was ecstatic over the gift of home-made pickle delivered Thursday last." They sat round the table in the reading room.

"It was really shocking, Professor. I swear to you, I saw this... this **living urn**."

"I recognise Clifford's book, of course. The distinctive cover, a haggy witch peering from behind a hedge. Sadly, he passed away last year. His widow keeps his urn of ash in the yellow caravan. But tell me are you on the verge of an investigation?"

"That outbreak of pumpkins on the church tower, pumpkins, to me, shout out loud HALLOWEEN, Halloween shouts out Grandma Nibbs."

"The old lady was known locally as a witch of the nasty kind."

"Nasty kind?"

"I observe you have a horseshoe hung above your cottage door, Betty."

"For luck," she laughed.

"Luck is an erroneous simplification. At one time, in this county alone, it was prudent to sacrifice a hen and bury it beneath the door stone. The horseshoe always pointing upwards was a protection against mysterious diseases and the power of the evil eye. Make no mistake, in those days old beldams, like Grandma Nibbs, were feared and respected."

"Can we please go and examine her grave? There might be some clues. Why, oh why should a witch, a dark witch, who was recently buried in the parish churchyard cause those pumpkins to grow all over the church tower. I'm certain it's her doing."

***

Betty, moving under the shade of a tall beech tree, noted the recently turfed, filled-in grave of Grandma Nibbs. Her funeral, it must be remembered, a modest affair, sparsely attended, though the weather atrociously stormy.

What was at odds, however, was a profusion of wild herbs rosemary, garlic, thyme and basil spreading across Grandma Nibbs grave. The growth of herbs more than apparent. Of interest to the junior sleuth was the neighbouring plot upon which growths of

Mrs Weevens

pumpkins had attempted but failed to root. The vines withered, the gourds shrivelled, tiny, skins mottled yellow covered in fungi. Careful not to tread on the actual grave, leaning forward, Betty was keen to study the old bald headstone. The name Weevens could just be made out.

On impulse, before even the professor could suggest, the girl was quick to snatch Clifford Tebbit's book out of her shoulder bag searching for the index page. Sure enough, Weevens got a mention on page 15. Mrs Weevens, as she was known, lived in the

seventeenth-century, to the great age of 103. A resident of Glim Glumswick all her life. Notable for healing powers, she was deeply loved by the farming community. She regularly dispensed potions and poultices, possessing a large herb garden, well-tended at her cottage.

One would refer to her, nowadays, as an apothecary, or a midwife, but here the resemblance must end, for none, including the Lord of the Manor, would dare cross her, or risk rebuke, for she was a witch, a white witch, capable of intoning spells.

"Professor?" the sound of Zmunxy's voice caused birds to flutter, a pair of squirrels watching events unfold from the treetops.

"I know what you mean to say Betty. Mrs Weevens is not well pleased, and Clifford also mentioned in his book the Glumswick Ley Line passes to the south of the tower – fascinating. We must of course advise the vicar and his sexton to rebury Grandma Nibbs some distance away on the other side of the churchyard. As the cockneys say, Grandma Nibbs is straying on to her turf, queering her pitch."

***

"The proper procedure for a reburial must be followed. The relevant authorities contacted. The next of kin informed. I'm so sorry, Professor, but your request for reinterment needs serious consideration. One cannot simply bundle a coffined body from one burial plot to another."

The professor nodded grimly. "Both of them are, or at least were in life, *witches*. Betty and I have already told you of our findings. To delay could have serious repercussions. Grandma Nibbs, a black practitioner, Mrs Weevens a white - both buried in close proximity. Their influence still felt."

"Oh dear, maybe it's all down to Ley Lines," joked the Reverend Smithson. "Rivalry from beyond the grave. That is, to me, rather a tall order. Is there not a more sensible explanation?"

"No," affirmed Betty, sipping her glass of orange squash kindly provided.

"Yet, I myself am unconvinced. You can never rush these things. I hear what you both say. However, it is not enough in my own mind to act further on the matter. The pumpkins are surely a horticultural freak of nature. I could never approach a church board on the basis of your witchcraft argument. Yes, I grant you, Grandma Nibbs, when alive, proved eccentric, her vengeful attitude towards P.C. Johns for arresting her son Alf, who served time on Dartmoor, reprehensible. But this woman, Mrs Weevens, also buried in our churchyard, existed in the seventeenth-century, for goodness sake. Really, no I'm sorry, we shall have to let the matter drop. The fire brigade are due to hack down the vines at the end of the week anyhow. I'm desperately sorry to disappoint you, Betty, but there we go. To give an example, you know that thunderstorm on the afternoon of Grandma Nibbs' funeral, the sky clouded over, went dark, we all had to dive under umbrellas, deluge of rain round the graveside. Lightning flashes, yet does that, in itself, indicate she was an evil witch? Is that enough evidence, or am I perhaps caving into superstition? Pray, think on that, the both of you."

Far from discouraged, Betty, still clutching her copy of Clifford Tebbit's book, focused on Mrs Staple's sweet shop and it was there, purchasing a threepenny ice lolly, she met Winnie White. Winnie argued in favour of the strange pumpkins wrapping themselves around the church tower and didn't care the slightest if they got bigger and the tower collapsed. There was nothing like a strawberry ice lolly and wafer ice cream to put things in perspective.

"Grandma Nibbs was always a bit weird though," Winnie agreed. "And she did have those hairy warts on her chin. But she's dead and gone, Betty. Forget about digging her back up. She's down there for good, composting the soil with the worms of England!"

Road to Christmas

One day Betty the clever schoolgirl sleuth ran her bicycle *not so cleverly* into a lamppost (or was it the lamppost ran into her) so sustaining a broken nose and a badly bruised jaw.

While her nose was being reset at Wellingford hospital, under anaesthetic, she underwent a weird change of place... for she seemingly hopped into a different time zone – shifting, as it were.

ZMunxy's eyes snapped open with a start. She was lying in a steel coffin. The damp, chill atmosphere made her realise the lid had mercifully been left off for it was propped up against the far wall.

Speaking of walls, it dawned upon her she was presently encased within four solid walls of a dungeon, built of stone slabs mildewed green and covered by spores of fungi. She perceived the tiny

hearth inbuilt into the wall was unlit, the grate extinct of coals and she started to shiver uncontrollably.

"Welcome to my Castle, I trust your stay with us will be short and not too uncomfortable. Ah, incidentally, this my wife the Queen."

Most profoundly was Betty struck by this odd couple. For in the dingy light afforded, she might assume ordinarily they were mother and child, he with his blonde, tidy hair, wearing a maroon frock

coat, diamond pinned kerchief and velvet pantaloons so tiny and small-boned, propped upon a type of high stool propelled by tiny casters. She tall, well over six feet in height, and slender, so pale did she seem, her skin might have been of the finest porcelain.

The Kings's wife, so tall and stately, her waxy white physiognomy queerly beautiful, allowed her abnormally rosy, red lips to part, revealing extremely sharp canines that creased her bottom lip when she smiled.

"Cripes, you are a vampire!" Betty enjoined.

"Both of us are vampires," The king corrected.

"But it is you who concerns us young lady, you are detained for good reason — the police reported 'riding without due care and attention, damaging a public lampost' other infringements, 'a loose saddlebag', 'poor air compression on your cycle pump', 'no puncture outfit', and what do you say to that?"

"Fiddlesticks, here's poor me being kept in a metal coffin."

"And I find that particular model looks so much more *streamlined* with the lid securely pressed down and vacuum sealed, wouldn't you agree, Queenly wife? But you just don't geddit do you missy."

"Am I to be buried alive then?"

"As a first offender we must be lenient, your punishment is to be sent into exile, to quit my principality forthwith. Exiled – do you hear me? You and your wretched rusty, flat-tyred bicycle sent packing to the furthest north, the land of endless snow, *the great ice plateau*. Fair weather or foul, it's the Pole you're headed for Miss. Oh, and my dear wife insisted your cloak be cleaned, chimney pot hat likewise brushed and those ankle boots of yours polished. The handle of your duck umbrella was a trifle loose, so we had it firmed up. As soon as the lid is secured, bon voyage, so to speak. You see, my dear, our species are really quite benevolent and much maligned."

***

The deep, deep cold penetrated her very being, confined, not in a stone dungeon, but a blue arched cavern some way down below the north pole. Apart from ventilation holes to allow a circulation of air, so at least she would not suffocate, the wretched metal lid the king had secured over her by means of a vacuum seal possessed a glass viewing window, so she was thus aware of her isolated, freezing environment.

Her face felt numb to the point where she must look not dissimilar to a frozen corpse.

How long have I been down here? She wondered, with so little room to shift her body. The King, the most cruel and unfeeling person she had ever met. Her fate – coffined inside an icicle infested cavern, Betty's senses alive to every nuance of her terrible predicament. She peered anxiously through the glass viewing window, up and up her gaze travelled.

The sheer, jagged face of the blue sheeted wall of

the crevasse funnelled upwards, suddenly a familiar

voice allowed to echo, due to the bouncy resonance.

Luckily help was close to hand. She could see her ghost mate Tudor Sefton in her vertical take-off coffin. The pilot manoeuvred her craft better than any kayak or canoe, descending the glacial wall – using her paddle brilliantly, stooping low before nudging her flying coffin into the icy cavern where

Betty lay alone. Her three-speed propped against the

far wall.

"'Bout time Tudor," Betty was so glad to see her best friend land gently on the blue gleaming ice. "How do I get out of this? The lid's sealed."

Tudor frowned for a bit, "Have you still got your duck handled umbrella?"

"Yeah."

"Lean against the upraised switch and when the compressor activates slide your umbrella – the curved handle – into the tiny gap, then you can break the vacuum seal."

Depressing the switch device Betty heard a clockwork whirring that wound down, followed by a noisy click - she could barely contain her joy, as the coffin lid, lifted with a sucking noise, she was free...

"Here grab a paddle - you've got a train to catch."

"Have I?"

"Back to Glim Glumswick silly."

With a lot of relief, Zmuxy clambered into Tudor's flying coffin and my means of vertical take-off they were soon flying under the stars.

"So where are we headed for this train - aren't we up in the North Pole - ooh, but it all does look so beautiful from up here - ever so Christmassy."

Betty paddled the magical kayak, timing her stroke to Miss Sefton's, warmed by the lamp on the

stick in the rear. "Doesn't Santa and all his snow elves and goblins have a present and wrapping paper factory down there?"

"Yeah, and a stable for his sleigh and reindeer don't forget," chuckled the coffin pilot - navigating by the green planet up above, making eventually a slow descent to the station precincts.

The departure board above indicated:

GLIM GLUMSWICK

VIA

BERING STRAIT

AND

BAFFIN ISLAND

DEPARTS 12.00

BOARDING

***

Betty was delighted to see a green locomotive waiting in the platform, hauling a couple of carriages. Amazingly her Raleigh bicycle had suddenly materialised, became brand new and cycled itself off to the luggage van, tinkling its bell.

The station itself, although completely made of ice, resembled those along the branch line she invariably encountered back home. Doors with signs like 'Waiting Room', 'Parcels Office', 'Ladies' and 'Gentlemen'.

Although the rooms themselves were visible from without, the verglas intricacy a marvel to behold, frozen solid and impossible to enter.

The translucent station canopy dripped a glittering array of icicles, prim window boxes, flower tubs, fire buckets, a cycle rack, porter's trolley…all exact replicas sculpted in ice.

Did she slide about on the glassy platform like a skating rink? No! she did not. Did the Great North Line engine belching smoke from its chimney, creating intense heat from the firebox, melt any part of the station.

Apparently not.

"Welcome. We leave right now. I have received via the grapevine an urgent telegraphic communication, a warning, Miss Zmunx, the police are wanting to detain a girl for serious cycling offences," barked the locomotive's metallic voice from the speaker grille positioned above the smoke-box door. "Have you on your travels perchance had dealings with the police before? I confess they will normally tend to prefer the warmer climes of the southern provinces. A policeman up here in the frozen north? Unheard of."

"Never mind that, let's head for Glim Glumswick."

"Cycling offences," chortled the locomotive, like a grinding lathe. "I'd like to see her cycling on this ice in these temperatures. Down she'd go, hitting the plateau like a lump of lead - clonk! Bike and all."

Boarding the train Betty was instantly part of a warm and cosy environment. It seemed to her a great burden had been lifted and, home bound, she was filled with happiness. She looked forward to her old familiar routine, the .... Oh, gracious, the memory of that detested King. It was true, she hated him - HATED HIM. But she just loved the green engine, so much so, she felt a song coming on.

The green engine gave a great blasting basso-hoot of whistle, and the train plunged into polar darkness.

Betty had the whole carriage to herself: a

foldaway sleeping bunk, a modest library of books, a writing desk, a plush and comfortable seat by the window, and a dining table laid with crisp, starched white cloth, glass, and silverware. A dumb waiter should supply all her meals and there was naturally a two-way speaker grille positioned above the serving hatch should she or the engine wish to communicate to each other. "Chummy chummy engine, chummy chummy engine, la la la." She sang happily.

"Chummy chummy engine, chummy chummy engine, ha ha ha." The engine was singing along, giving a toot, toot, toot with it's whistle, adding wind accompaniment.

***

"Can you hear me, Betty? Squeeze my finger – ooch! Not that hard, matron, her eyes are opening, do come and look.

"Would you believe it," laughed the doctor.

The girl's eyes did open. She was aware of plain magnolia emulsioned ceiling, hooded electric lamps, half tiled sterile white wall and the smell of antiseptic. There was a large window looking over a parking space on an overcast day. It was sleeting, her whole face felt numb.

***

The intervening period between school break up - and Christmas passed uneventfully.

The day before Christmas Eve, although it was far more likely for the village to be swept by gales and torrential rain, that year it snowed heavily and the whole of Glim Glumswick got a good covering.

Pavements, roads, gardens, rooves of house's, along the high street received two or three inches at least. Due to a severe frost that night and a dip in daytime temperatures (although no more snow was forecast) patchy areas in effect hung around, giving gardens in Old Partridge Lane a white-ish festive outlook. Even if that meant on Christmas Day itself just a heaping of grubby snow round by the bird table, a lump or two dolloped on the lawn or a dusting on the shed roof, that was better than none at all.

The bitter cold temperatures were not to everyone's liking but persisted throughout Christmas.

On Christmas eve, after midnight carol service. Betty taught mother and aunt Medley a new melody. Toes were seen tapping, hips swaying.

The cottage felt warm and inviting, a coal fire flickered contentedly in the grate behind the mesh fireguard, the mantelpiece mum had sanded and painted magnolia gloss a couple of weeks previous

decorated with sprigs of holly and crinkly paper bells, the ceiling strung with a colourful variety of home-made paper chains, the loops cut out and gummed by the family.

In the corner was a Norwegian spruce from the covered market. Brown paper packages were heaped round the tub, itself wrapped in a single sheet of bright red crépe-paper.

Bottles of Harvey's and Croft Original, along with

plates of walnuts and tangerines placed on an oval table once belonging to Betty's grandmother Maud.

The steady heat from the kitchen stove kept the downstairs warm, and paraffin heaters kept them comfortable upstairs despite the bitterly cold night-time temperatures.

Betty got so carried away with last minute shopping, gadding about the closed market, present wrapping, she was unsuspecting of darker, more sinister undertones waiting patiently for a time and place to strike at their most ferocious. Mother and aunt Medley had gone to bed. She leaned down to plump Berties tartan blanket in the wicker dog basket and, looking about one last time, Thrilled beyond measure.

Upon re-entering the sitting room, her whole, festive world crumbled.

She was but a tiny worm wriggling helplessly in the beak of a hungry black crow.

The dreaded squeak of a highchair on castors gave way to a sinking sense of doom, an abrupt curtailment of all that was happy and free and wonderful.

The King of the castle, his round, cherubic face glowing by the firelight, occupied one side of the homely hearth and his horse-faced, tall, and intimidating vampire of a wife, the other.

The king bared his sharp fangs in a feral snarl of utter contempt as Betty cowered in the corner over by the Christmas tree.

"A very, merry olde Christmas to you, Miss Betty, the Queen and I wish you continued festive joy, with the proviso that when you are exiled to the Great Plateau next time, you stay there!"

The coal fire reacted by flames bursting up the chimney as though hastily beating a retreat from the pair.

"How cruel you people are!" Betty commented.

"Cruel, cruel, cruel – you can get lost."

"FAIR, not cruel," the king corrected her, leaning forward in his highchair, his voice rising an octave as he sought to set out the facts as he saw them. "Go back – wilful criminal damage to a lampost, the police pointing out – ineffective bicycle pump action,

saddle bag loose, no puncture outfit, all of these serious offences."

"I Don't Care."

The King sniggered. "Now, we shall materialise the steel coffin over by your twinkling tree and be on our way. Once you are safely contained and secure, you shall depart this night for the North. We wish your festive Christmas decorations a fond farewell - no!"

"What about a reduced sentence, I deserve it, I came top in maths." Said Zmunxy. "It is Christmas after all."

The Queen intervened for she had taken quite a shine to the girl and admired her pluck.

"Oh, great and mighty King, think again for my sake."

"Very well," said he haughtily. "We, will spare you untold torture, misery, and lengthy confinement in the steel coffin.

Be grateful that we, the King and Queen find the terms of your reduced sentence thus… We impose a fine of one bag of gold coin. Failure to deposit this amount into our coffers now will result in reverting to former sentencing." He sneered at Betty and then cast a crafty glance at his wife, whose long, horsey face with its prominent cheekbones, became that much more horrible in the firelight as she waited to see Betty's reaction.

"How long do I have to procure this bag of gold?" she demanded to know.

"Two minutes." Still reeling from this utter cruelty, even at this late stage the man was capable of downright nastiness.

Looking about her, she deduced a masterly idea, thus snatching a convenient novelty bag of chocolate gold coins from a branch off the Christmas tree she handed them in, hopeful the king would not even notice the difference.

They rattled realistically enough and now growling under his breath, begrudgingly he

accepted the payment and pocketed the gold coins forthwith in his velvet jacket. Then the pair vanished into thin air.

CHOCOLATE had won the day, chocolate ruled and
that's how it should be.

"Merry Christmas" said Aunt Medley.

"Happy Christmas," said mother.

"Happy Christmas," replied Betty.

They all sang and danced to Betty's catchy tune;
the one Aunt Medley had been humming all
morning.

Song lyrics by Betty and the Green Engine:

Chummy, chummy engine,

Chummy chummy engine,

La, la, la.

Chummy, chummy engine,

Chummy chummy engine

Ha, ha, ha.

Chummy, chummy engine,

Chummy chummy engine

Toot, toot, toot.

(repeat and repeat chorus)

Characters in the series